The woods are a peaceful place, but when a crime is committed Rory the tiger and Sheldon the turtle don their masks and capes and—

POW! WHAM! KABAM!

—become Super Rory and Super Sheldon . . .

THE SUPER-DUPER DUO

www.hmhco.com

ISBN: 978-1-328-76678-6

Manufactured in China
SCP 10 9 8 7 6 5 4 3 2 1
4500660190

THE SUPER-DUPER DUO

A BEARY MERRY CHRISTMAS

Story by Henri Meunier Illustrated by Nathalie Choux
Adapted by Liza Charlesworth

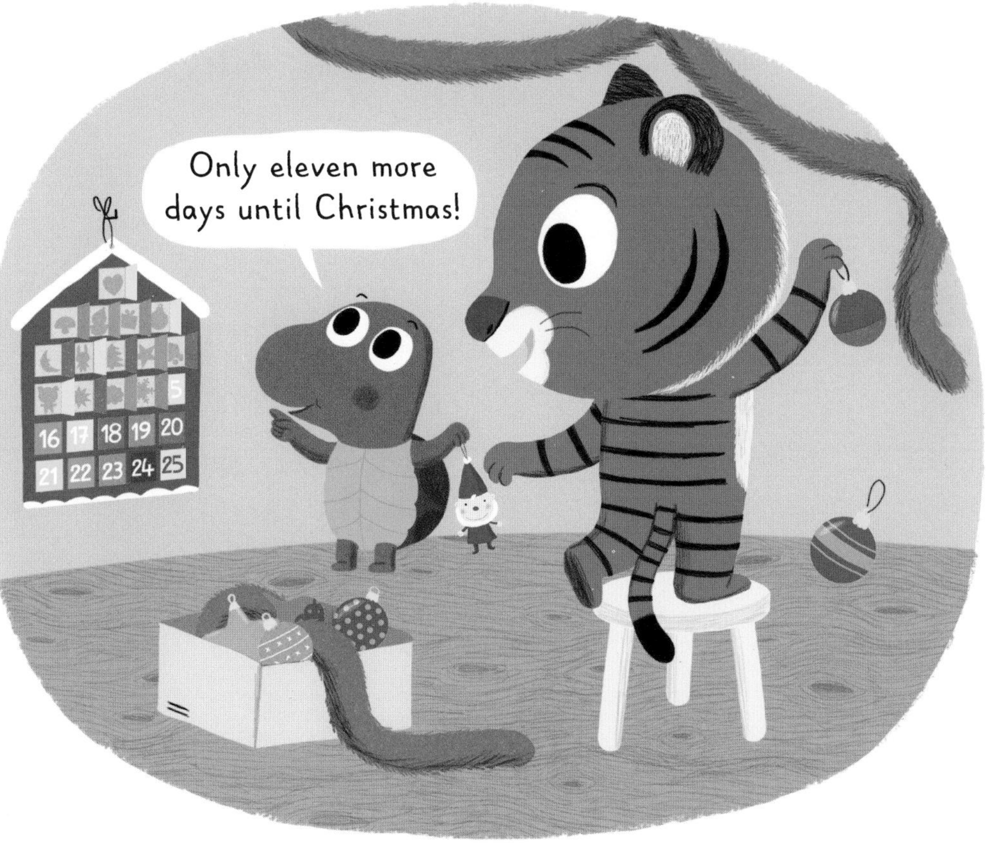
Only eleven more days until Christmas!
16 17 18 19 20
21 22 23 24 25

Houghton Mifflin Harcourt
Boston New York

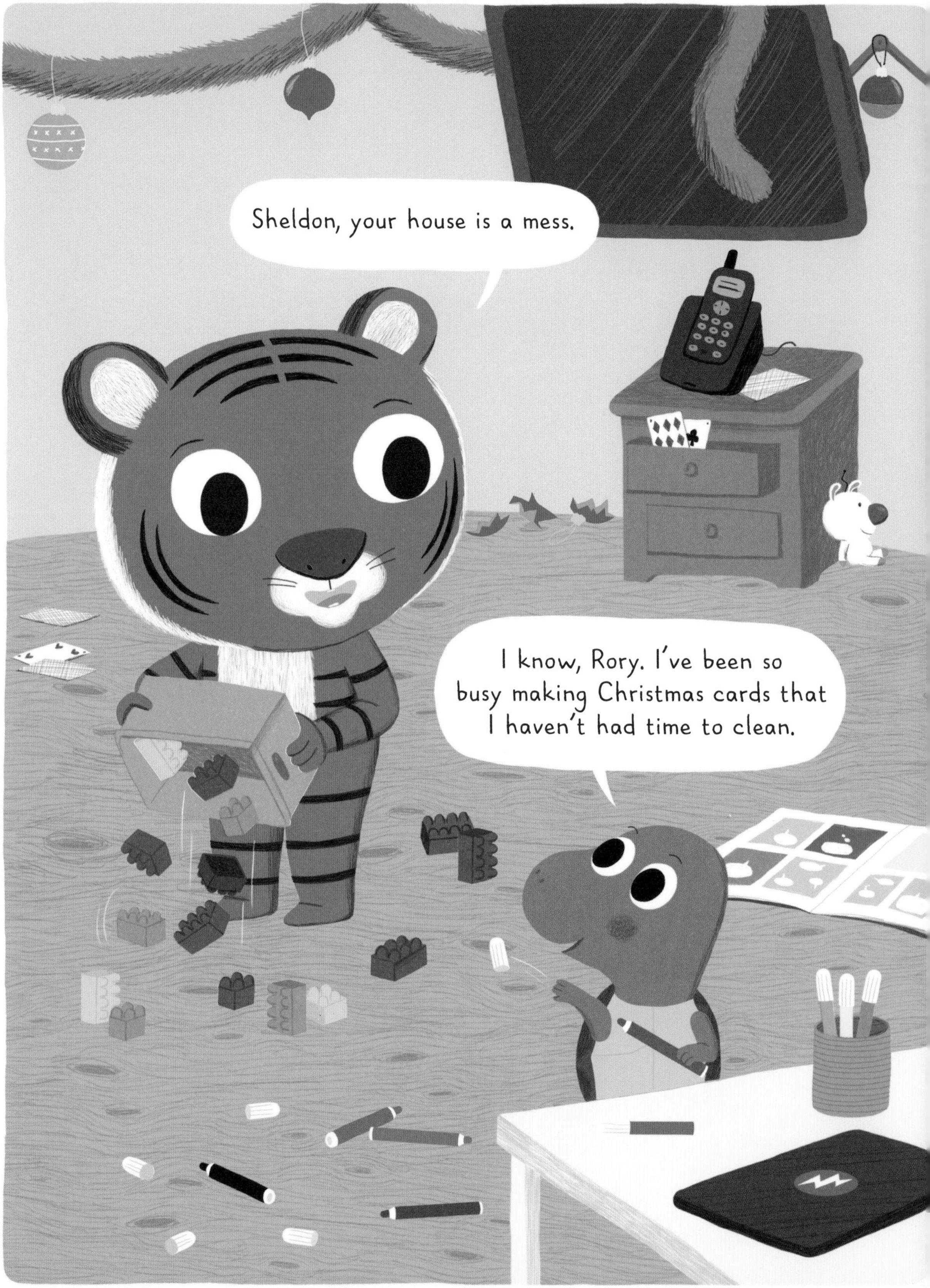
Sheldon, your house is a mess.
I know, Rory. I've been so busy making Christmas cards that I haven't had time to clean.

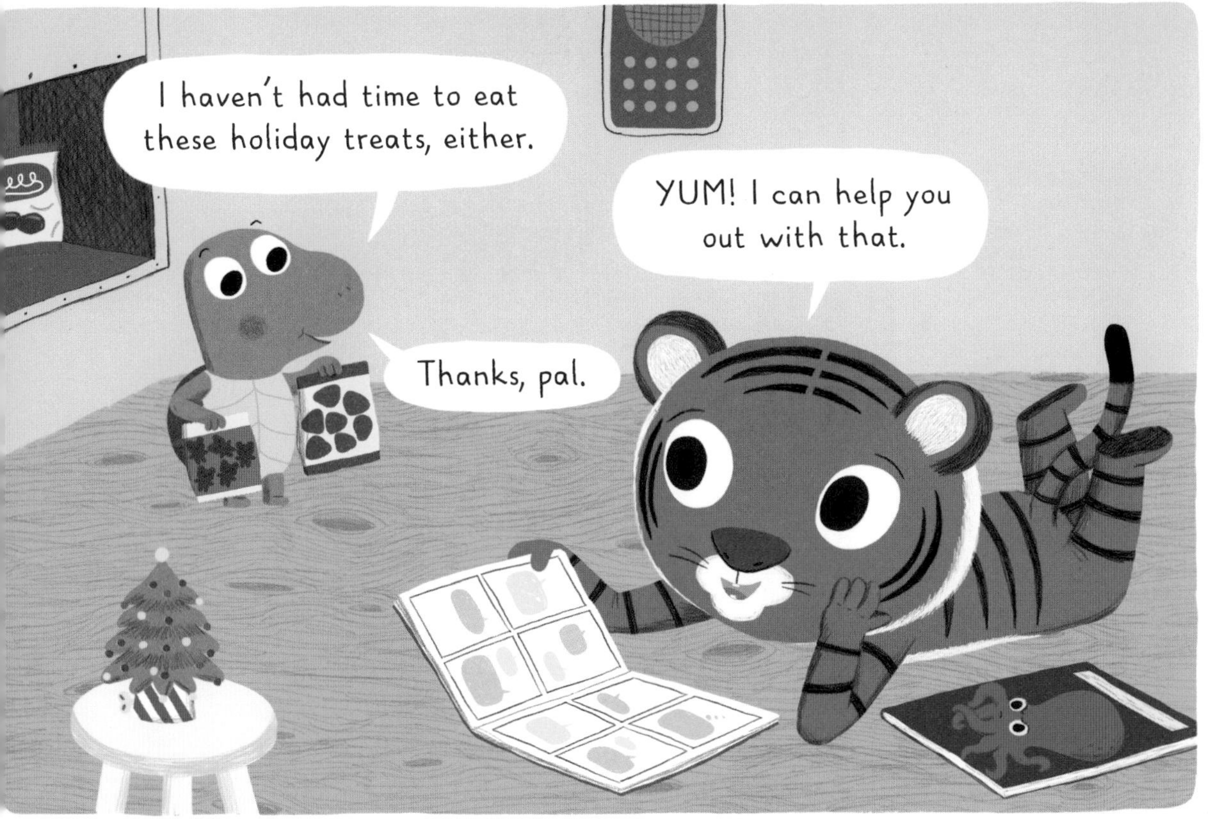
I haven't had time to eat these holiday treats, either.
YUM! I can help you out with that.
Thanks, pal.

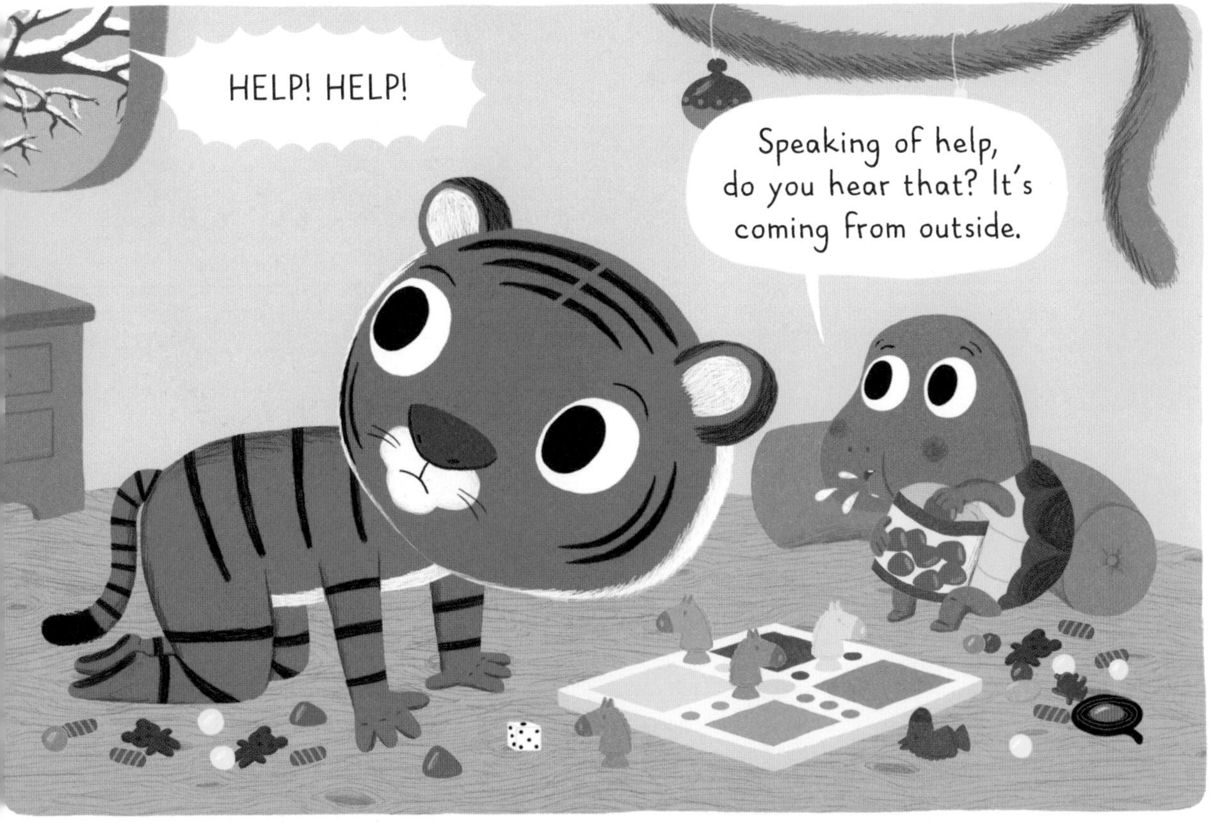
HELP! HELP!
Speaking of help, do you hear that? It's coming from outside.

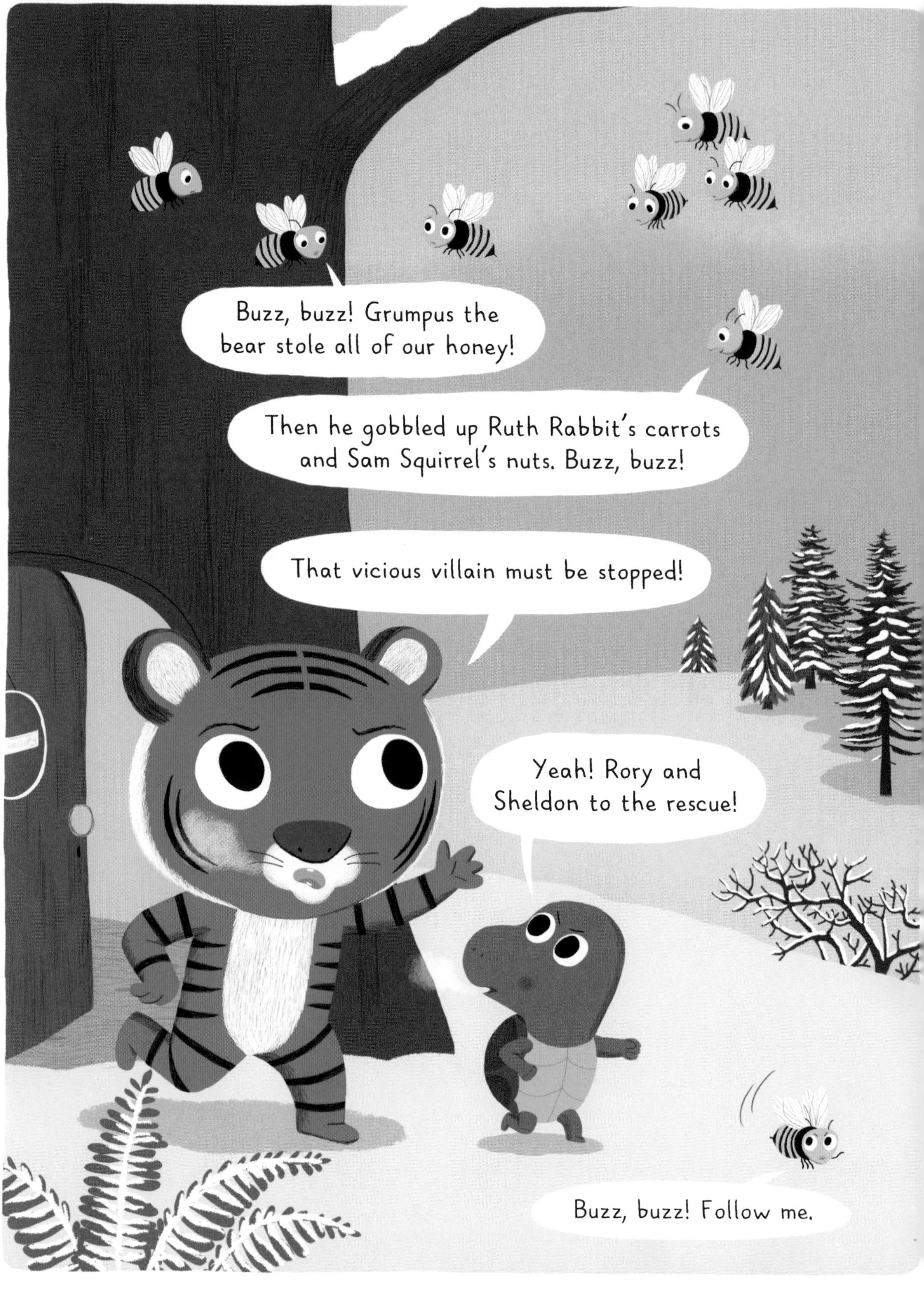
Buzz, buzz! Grumpus the bear stole all of our honey!
Then he gobbled up Ruth Rabbit's carrots and Sam Squirrel's nuts. Buzz, buzz!
That vicious villain must be stopped!
Yeah! Rory and Sheldon to the rescue!
Buzz, buzz! Follow me.

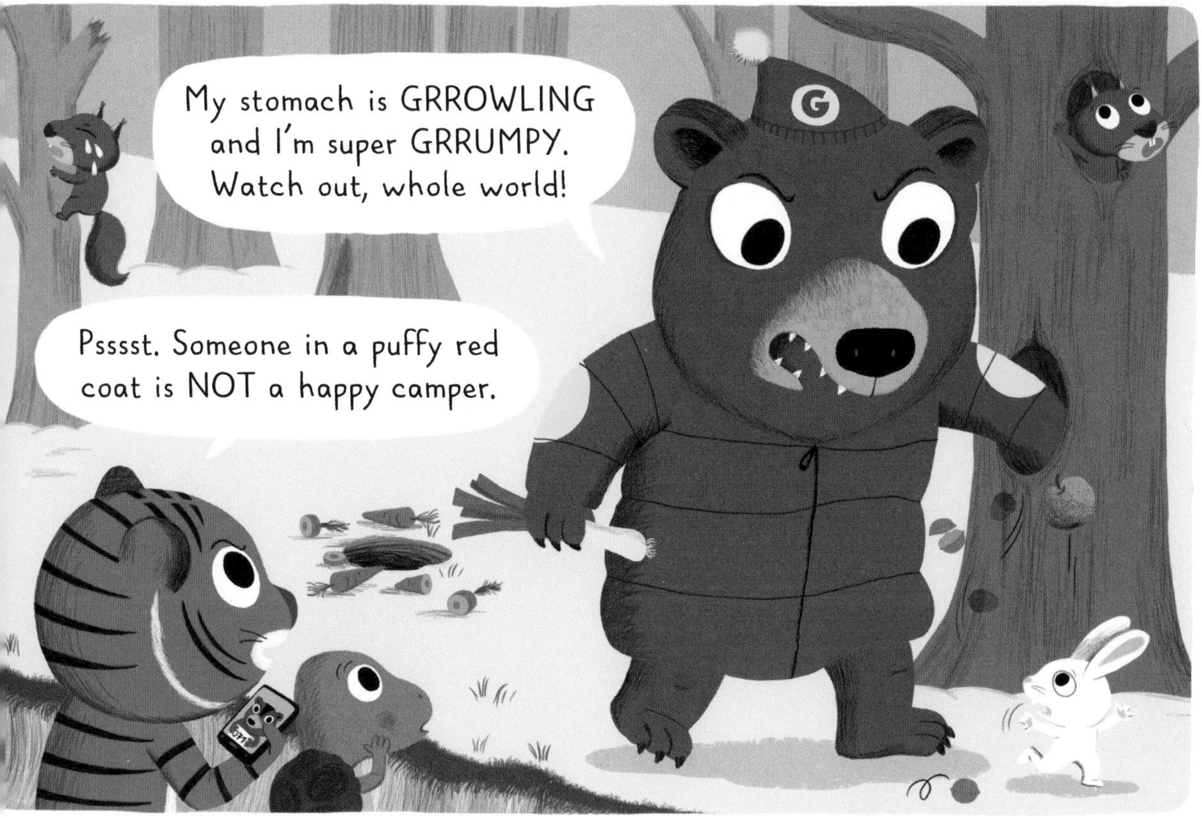
My stomach is GRROWLING and I'm super GRRUMPY. Watch out, whole world!
Psssst. Someone in a puffy red coat is NOT a happy camper.
911

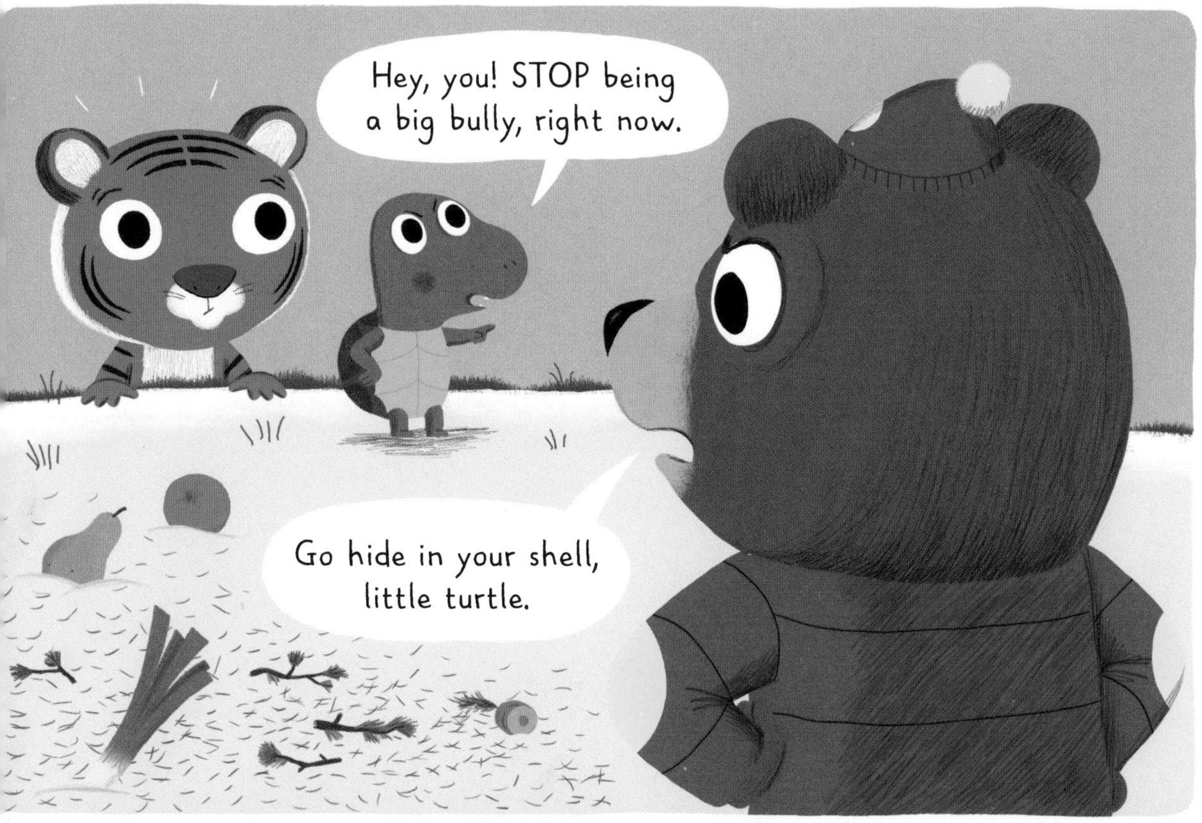
Hey, you! STOP being a big bully, right now.
Go hide in your shell, little turtle.

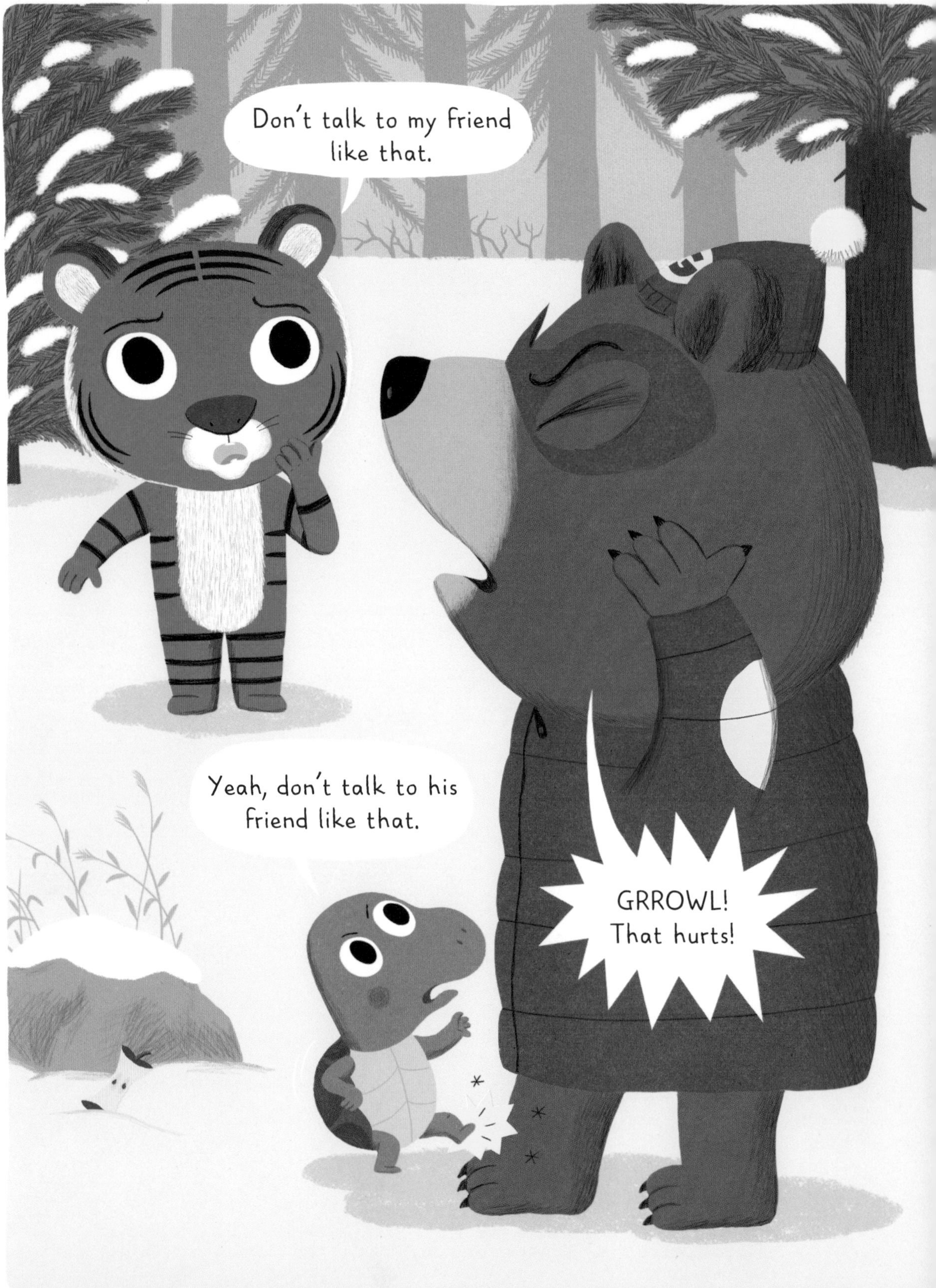
Don't talk to my friend like that.
Yeah, don't talk to his friend like that.
GRROWL! That hurts!

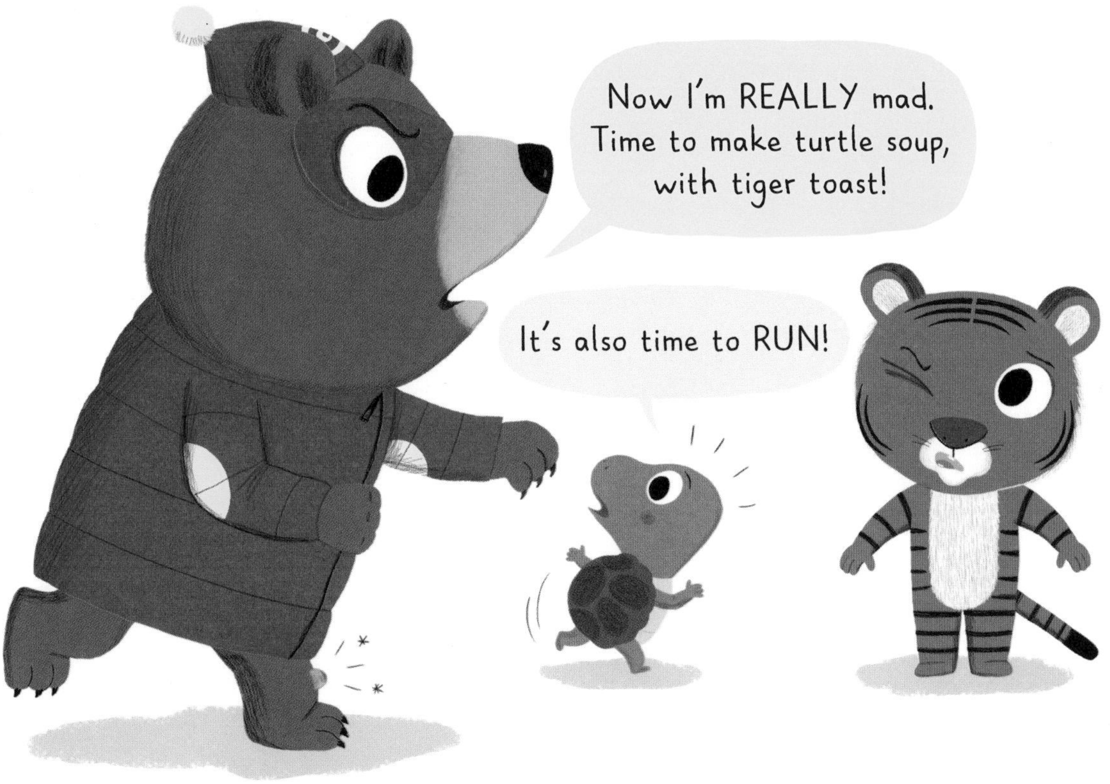
Now I'm REALLY mad. Time to make turtle soup, with tiger toast!
It's also time to RUN!

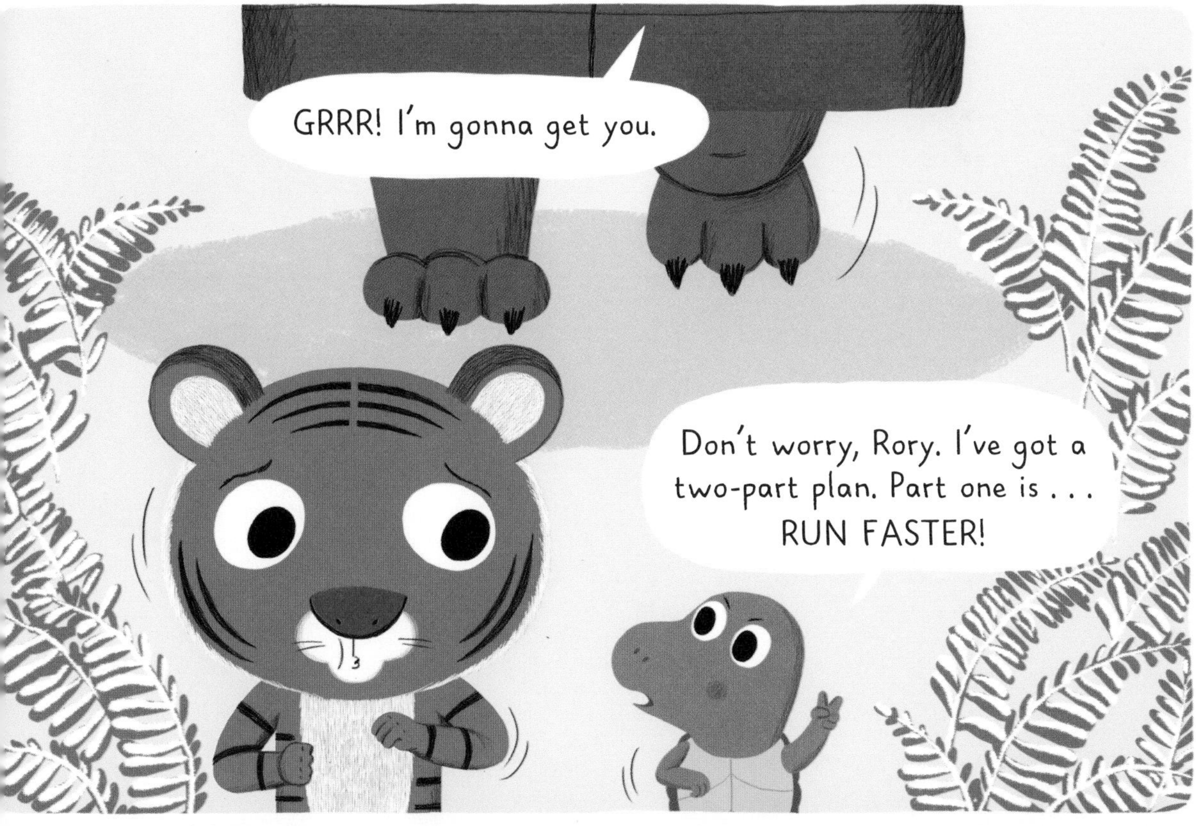
GRRR! I'm gonna get you.
Don't worry, Rory. I've got a two-part plan. Part one is . . . RUN FASTER!

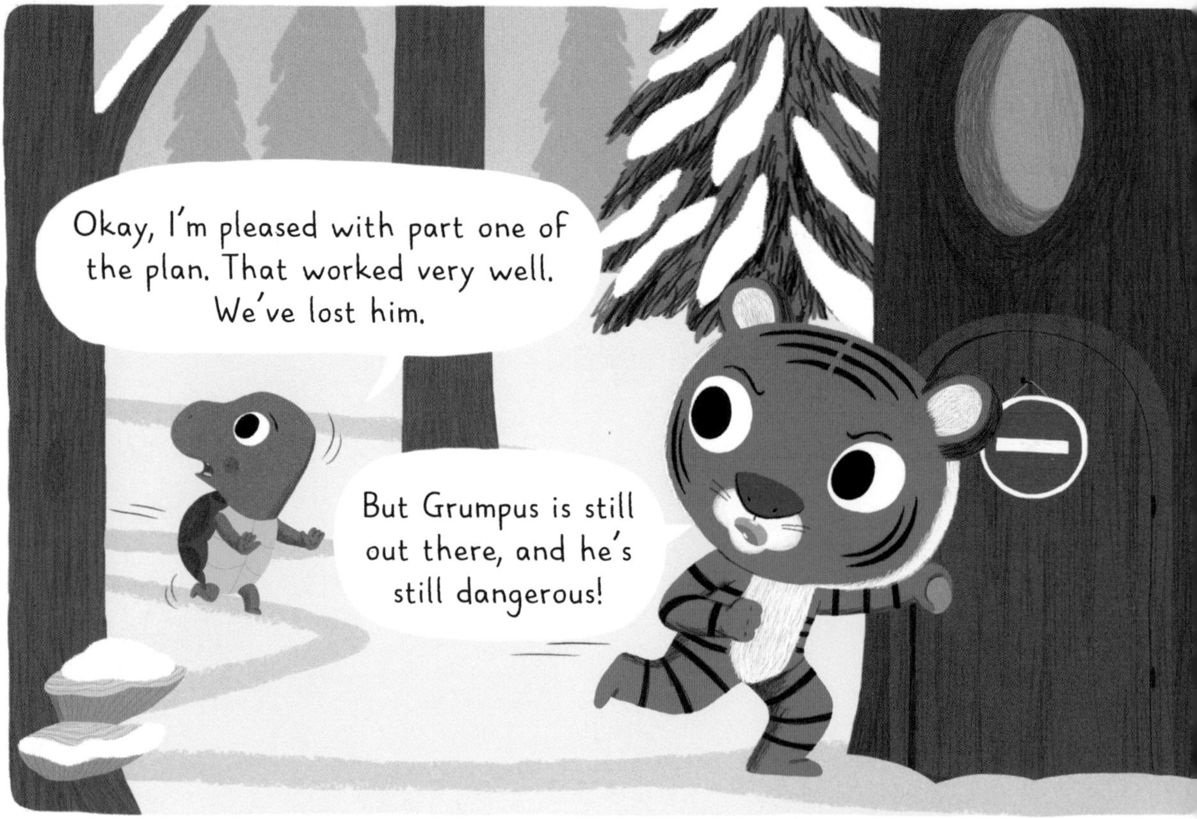
Okay, I'm pleased with part one of the plan. That worked very well. We've lost him.
But Grumpus is still out there, and he's still dangerous!

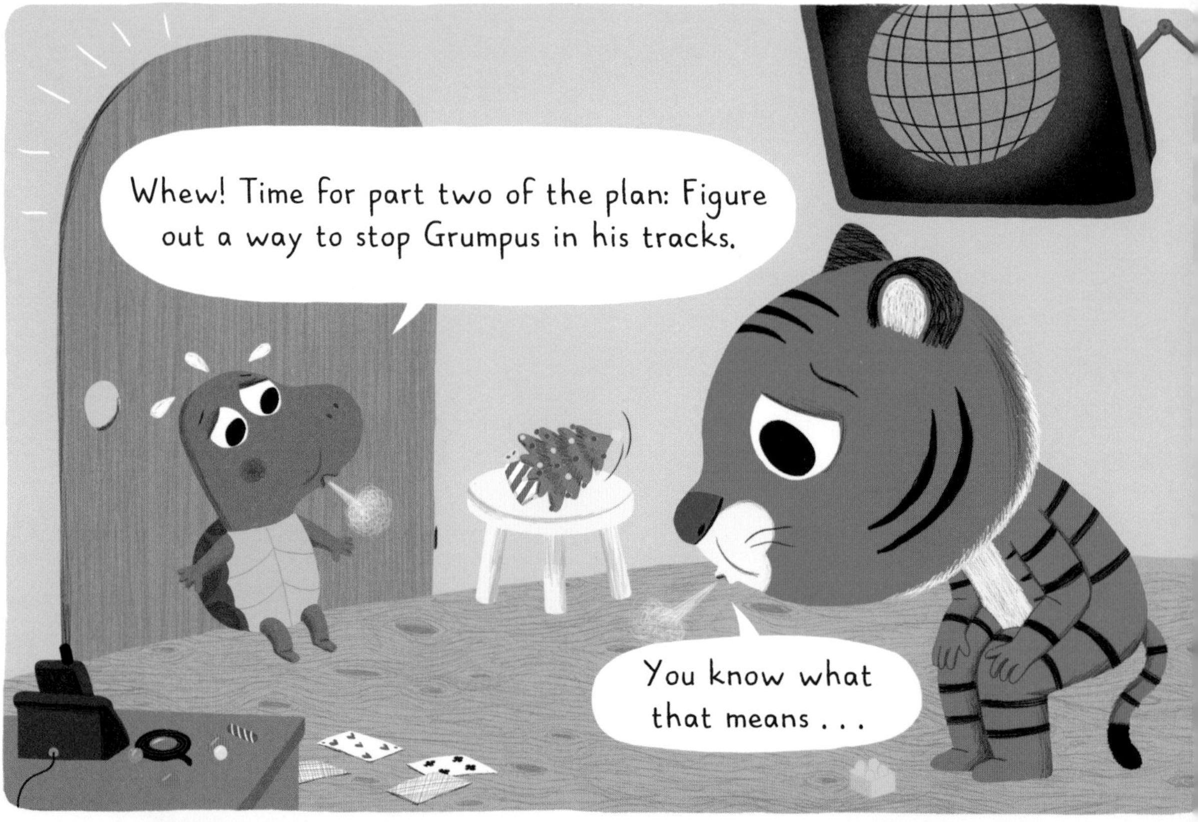
Whew! Time for part two of the plan: Figure out a way to stop Grumpus in his tracks.
You know what that means . . .

Time to change into our crime-fighting gear.
POW!
WHAM!
KABAM!
Super-Duper Duo to the rescue!

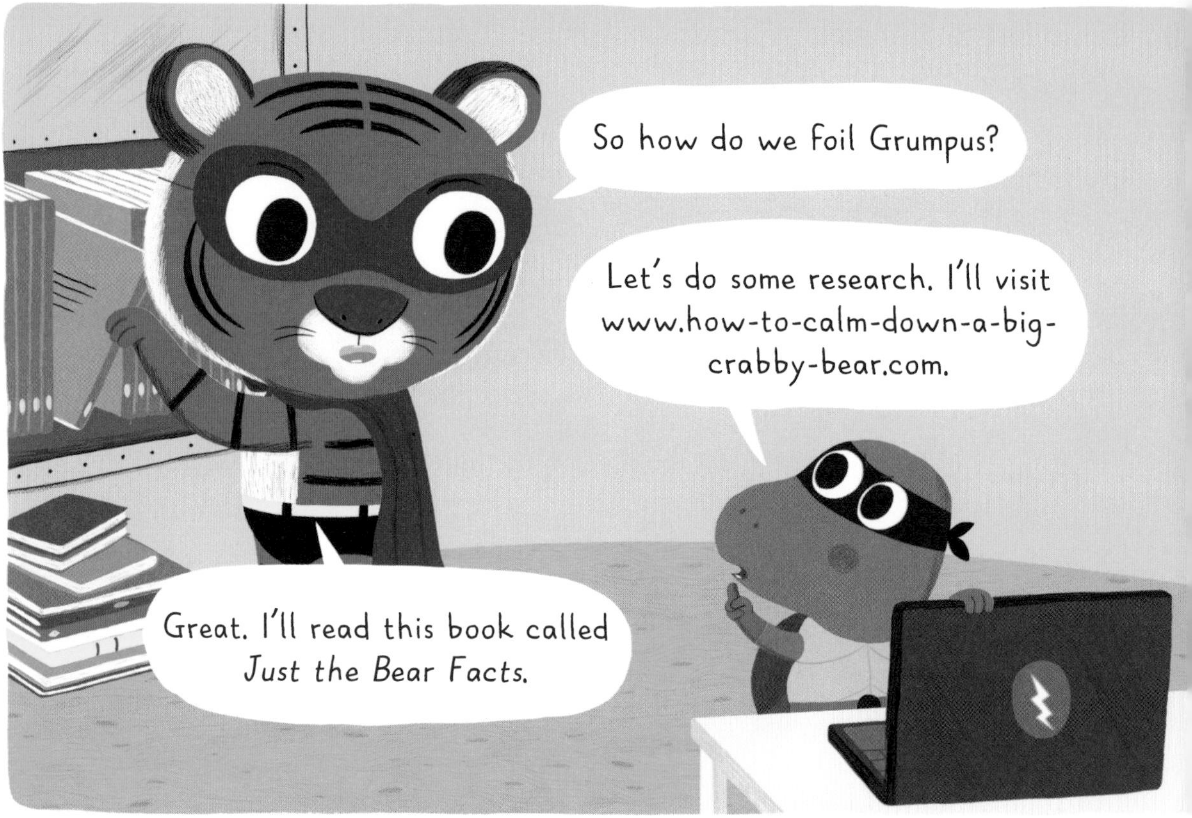
So how do we foil Grumpus?
Let's do some research. I'll visit www.how-to-calm-down-a-big-crabby-bear.com.
Great. I'll read this book called *Just the Bear Facts*.

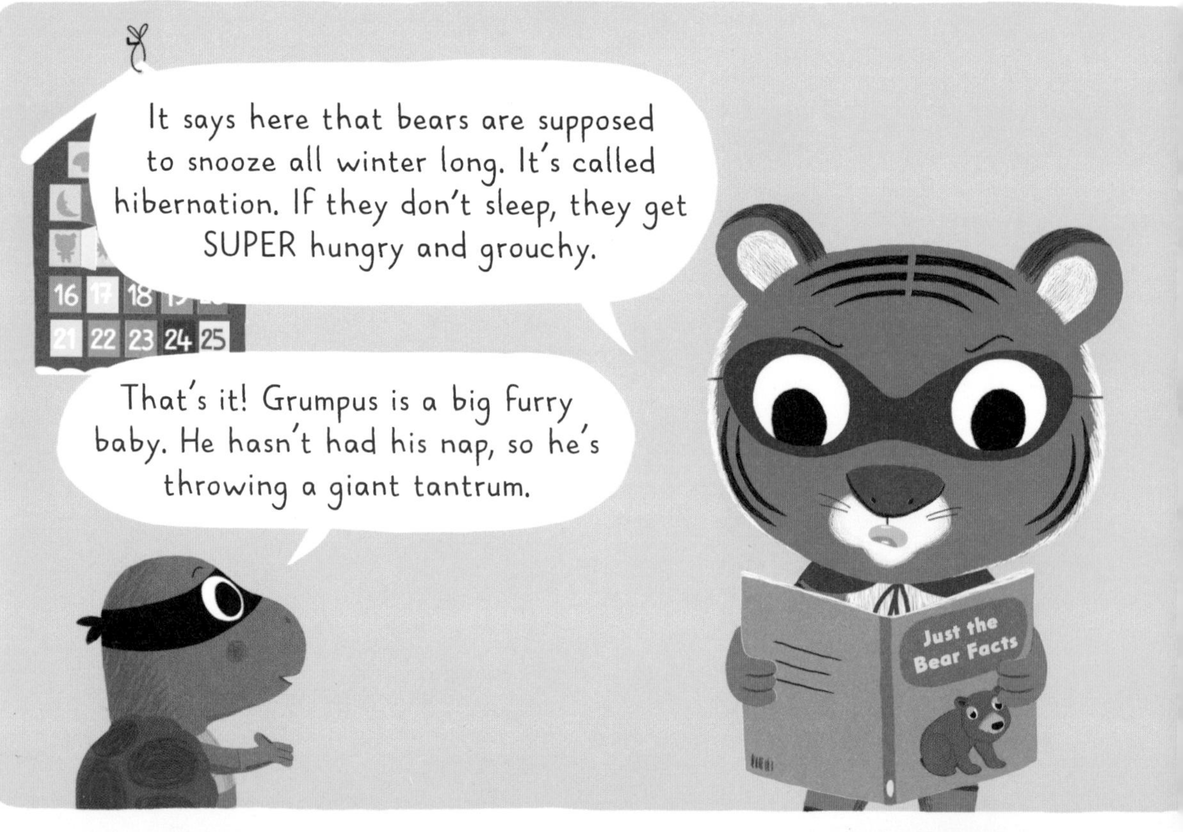
It says here that bears are supposed to snooze all winter long. It's called hibernation. If they don't sleep, they get SUPER hungry and grouchy.
That's it! Grumpus is a big furry baby. He hasn't had his nap, so he's throwing a giant tantrum.
Just the Bear Facts

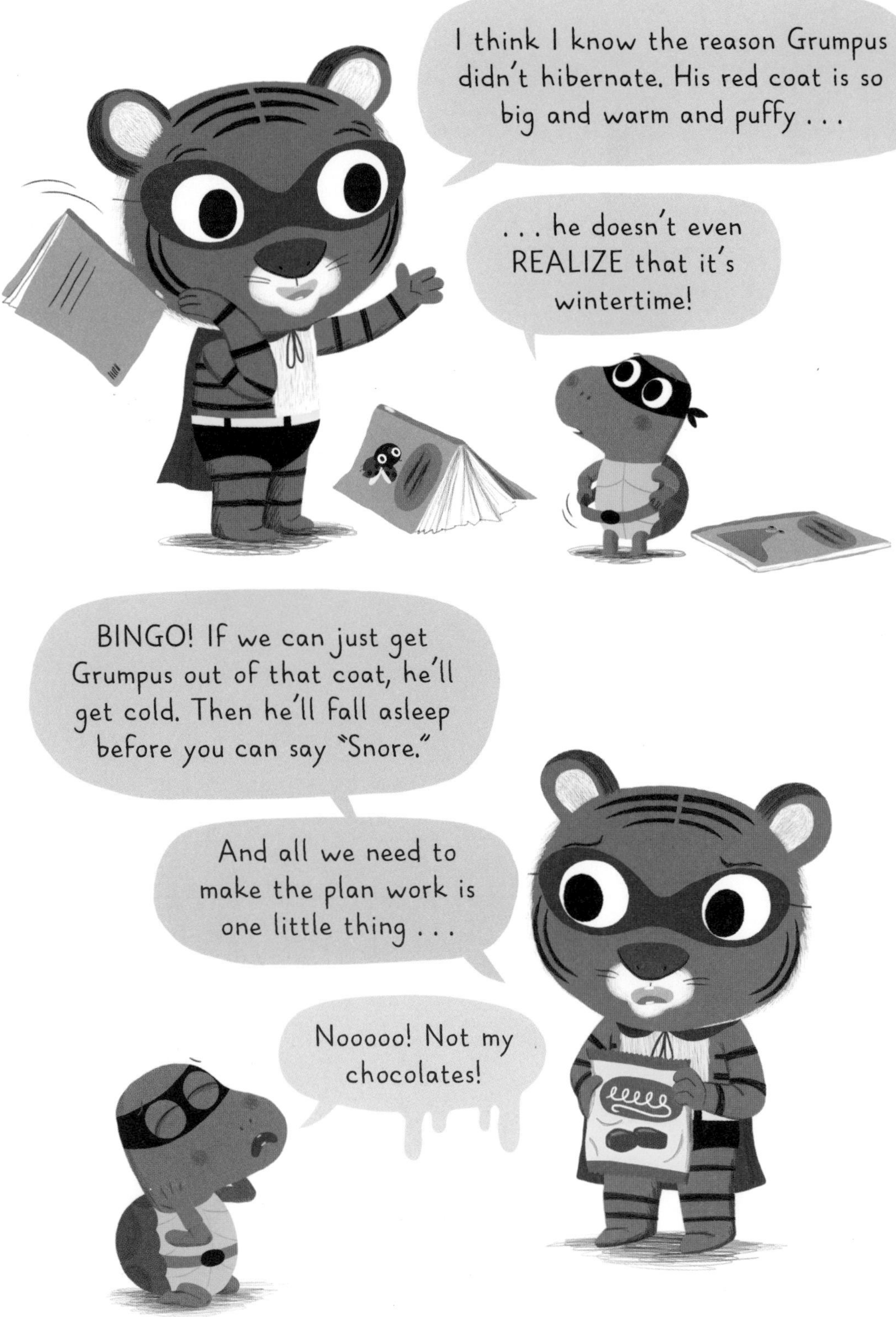
I think I know the reason Grumpus didn't hibernate. His red coat is so big and warm and puffy . . .
. . . he doesn't even REALIZE that it's wintertime!
BINGO! If we can just get Grumpus out of that coat, he'll get cold. Then he'll fall asleep before you can say "Snore."
And all we need to make the plan work is one little thing . . .
Nooooo! Not my chocolates!

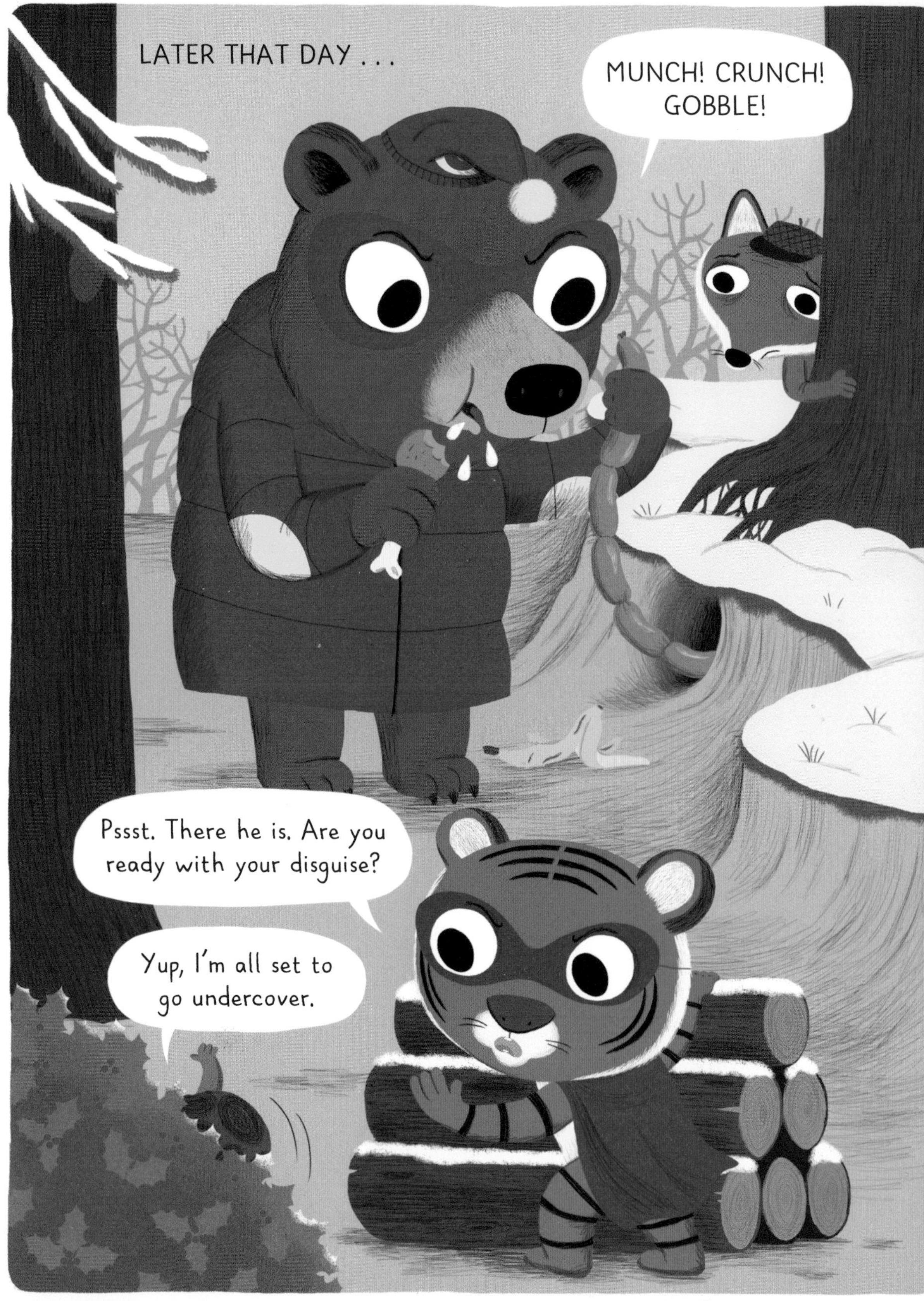
LATER THAT DAY . . .
MUNCH! CRUNCH! GOBBLE!
Pssst. There he is. Are you ready with your disguise?
Yup, I'm all set to go undercover.

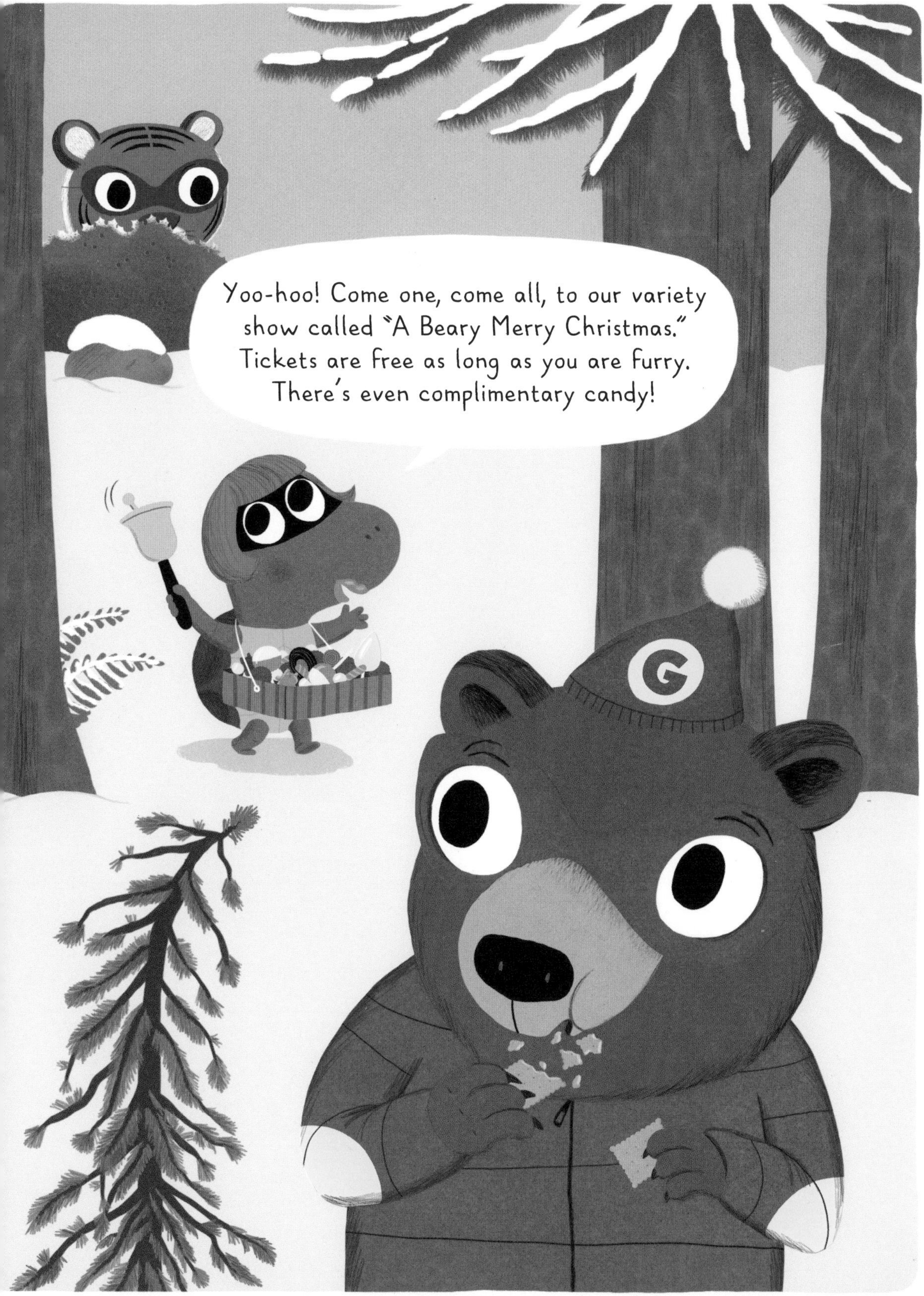
Yoo-hoo! Come one, come all, to our variety show called "A Beary Merry Christmas." Tickets are free as long as you are furry. There's even complimentary candy!

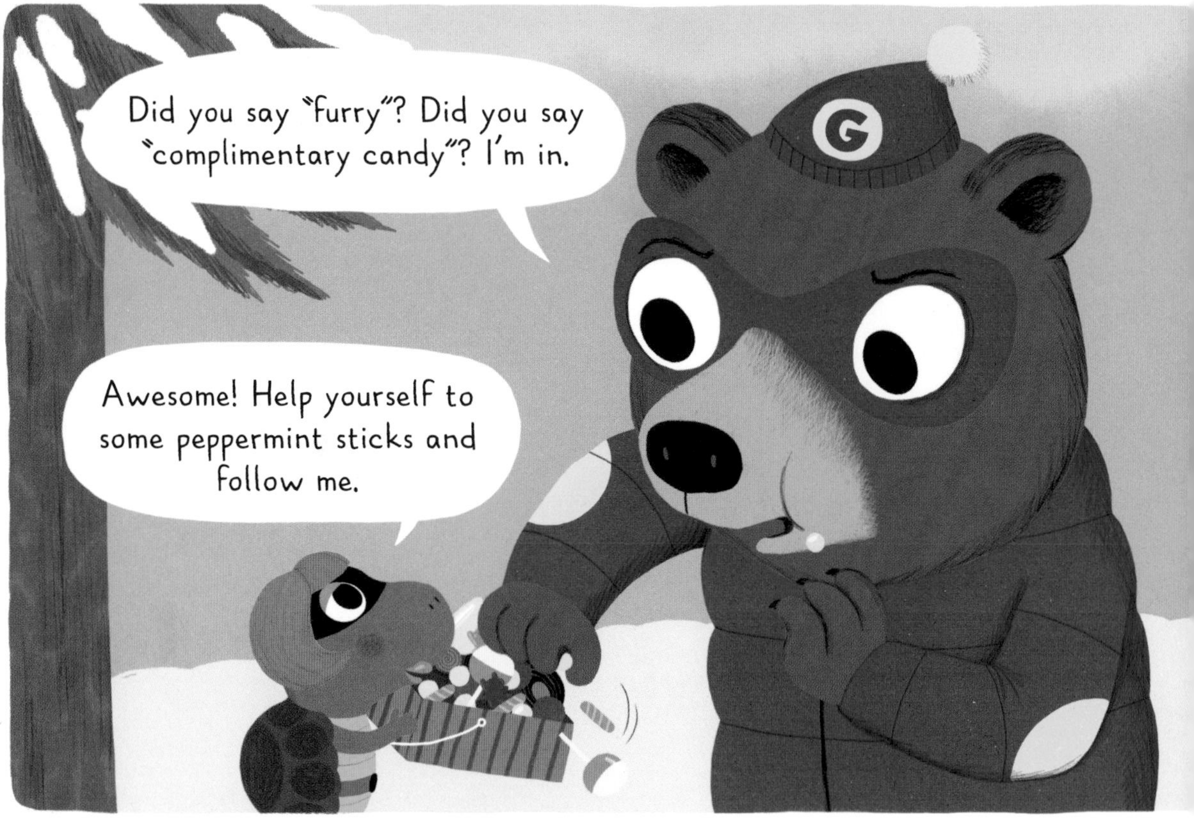
Did you say "furry"? Did you say "complimentary candy"? I'm in.
Awesome! Help yourself to some peppermint sticks and follow me.

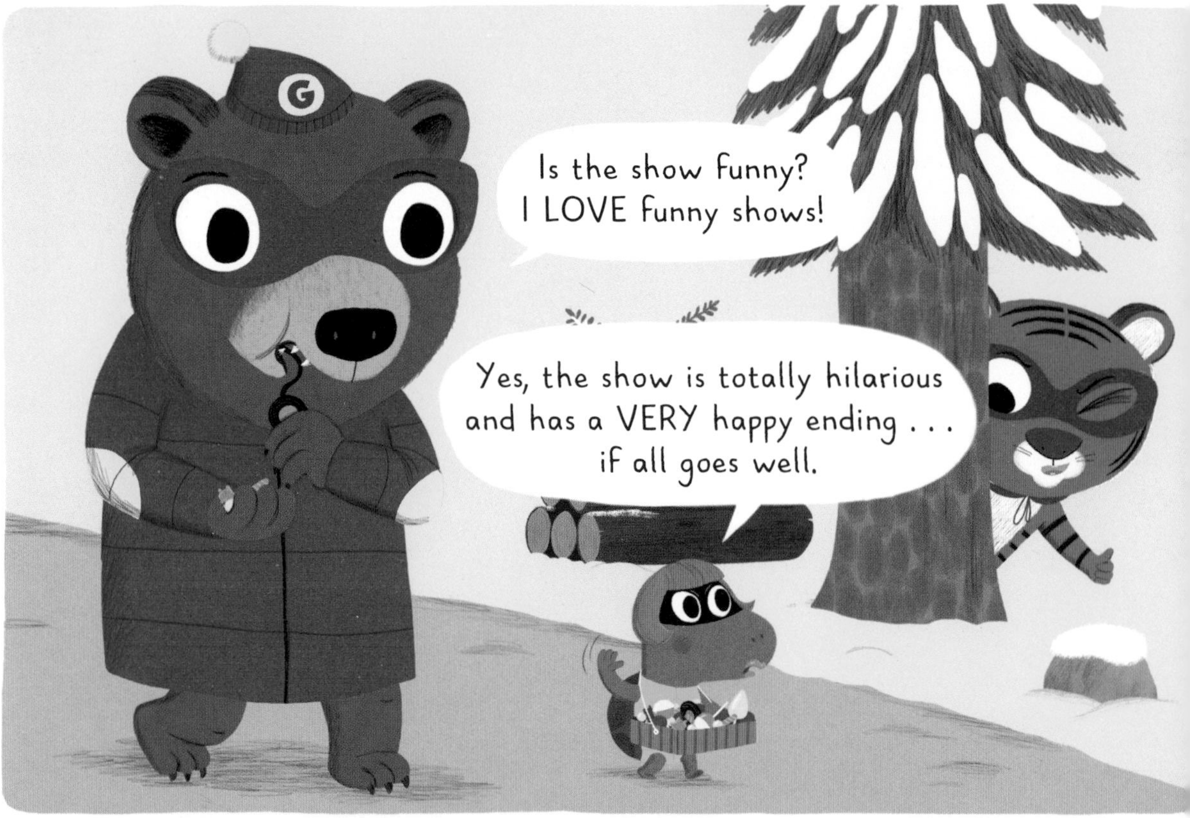
Is the show funny? I LOVE funny shows!
Yes, the show is totally hilarious and has a VERY happy ending . . . if all goes well.

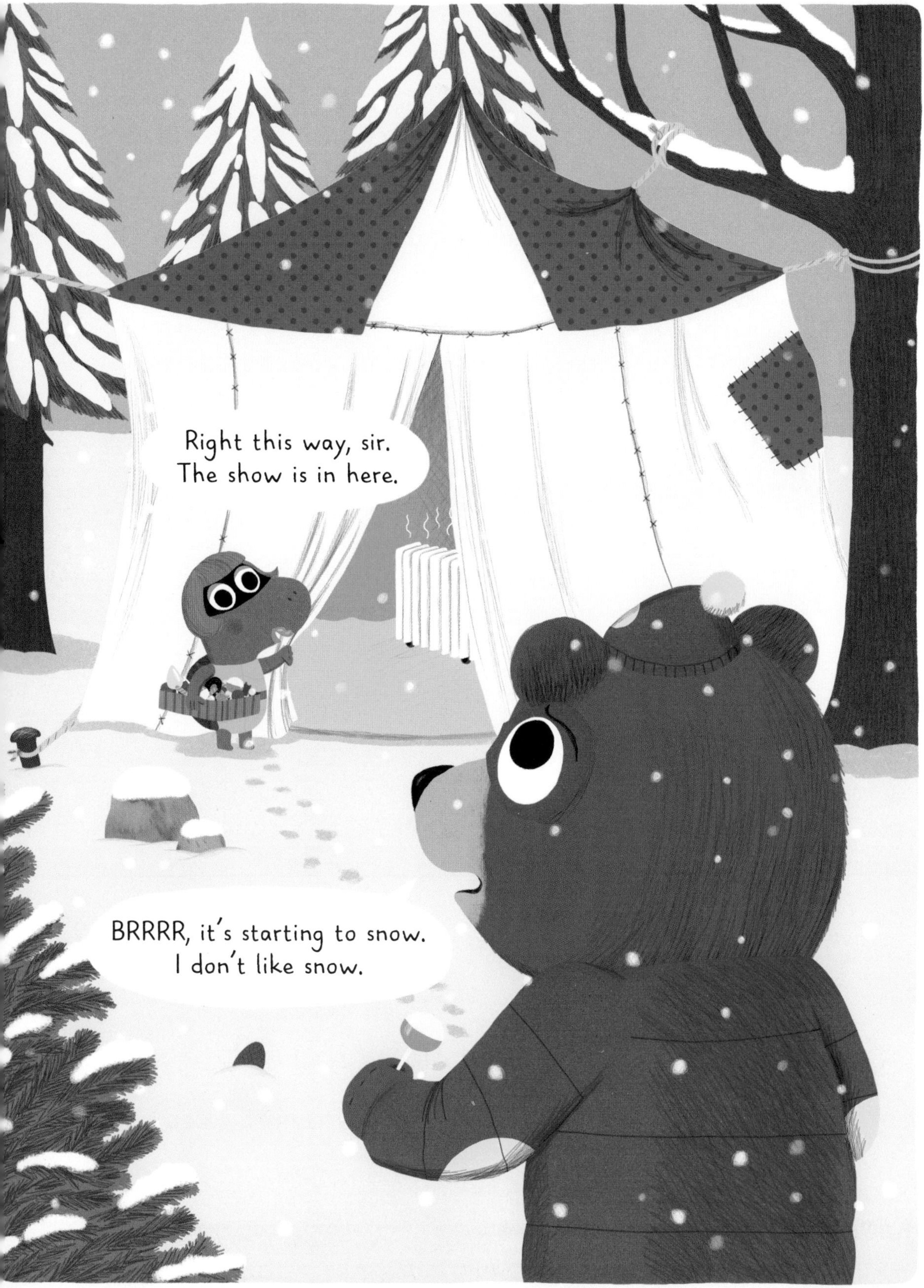
Right this way, sir. The show is in here.
BRRRR, it's starting to snow. I don't like snow.

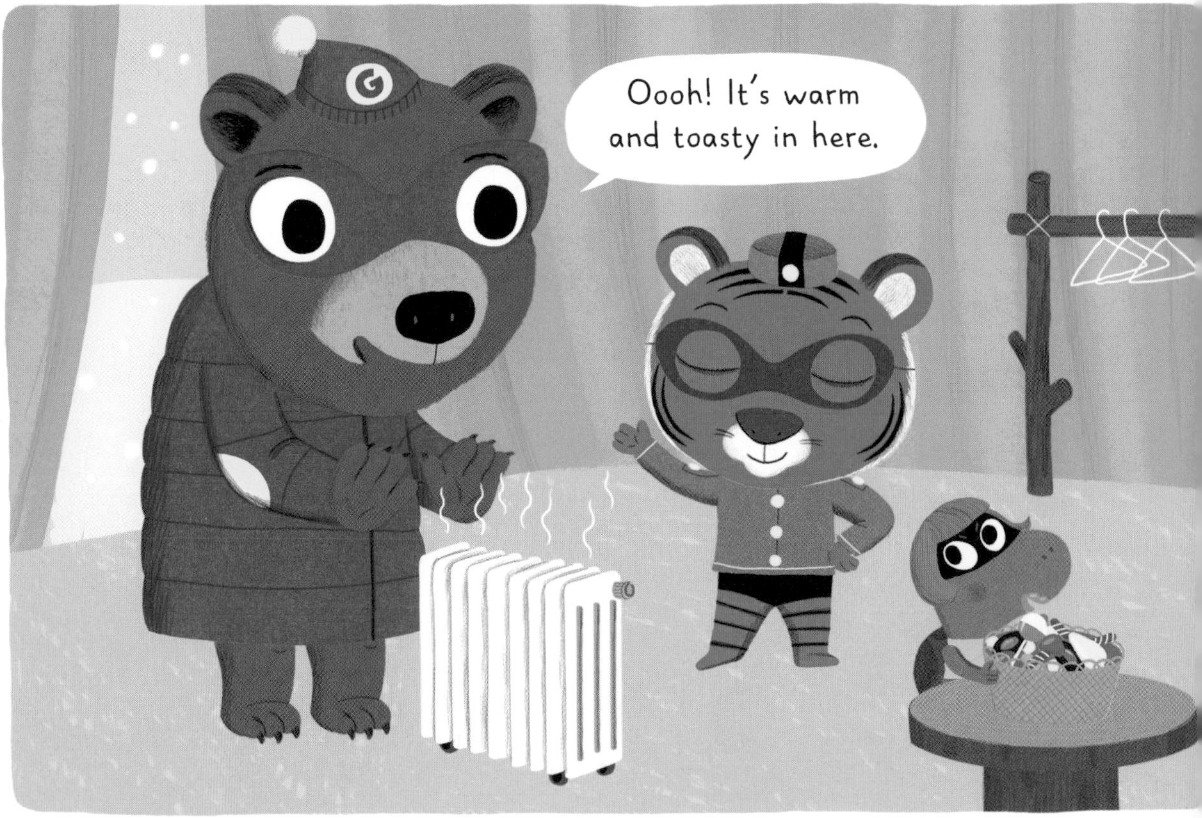
Oooh! It's warm and toasty in here.

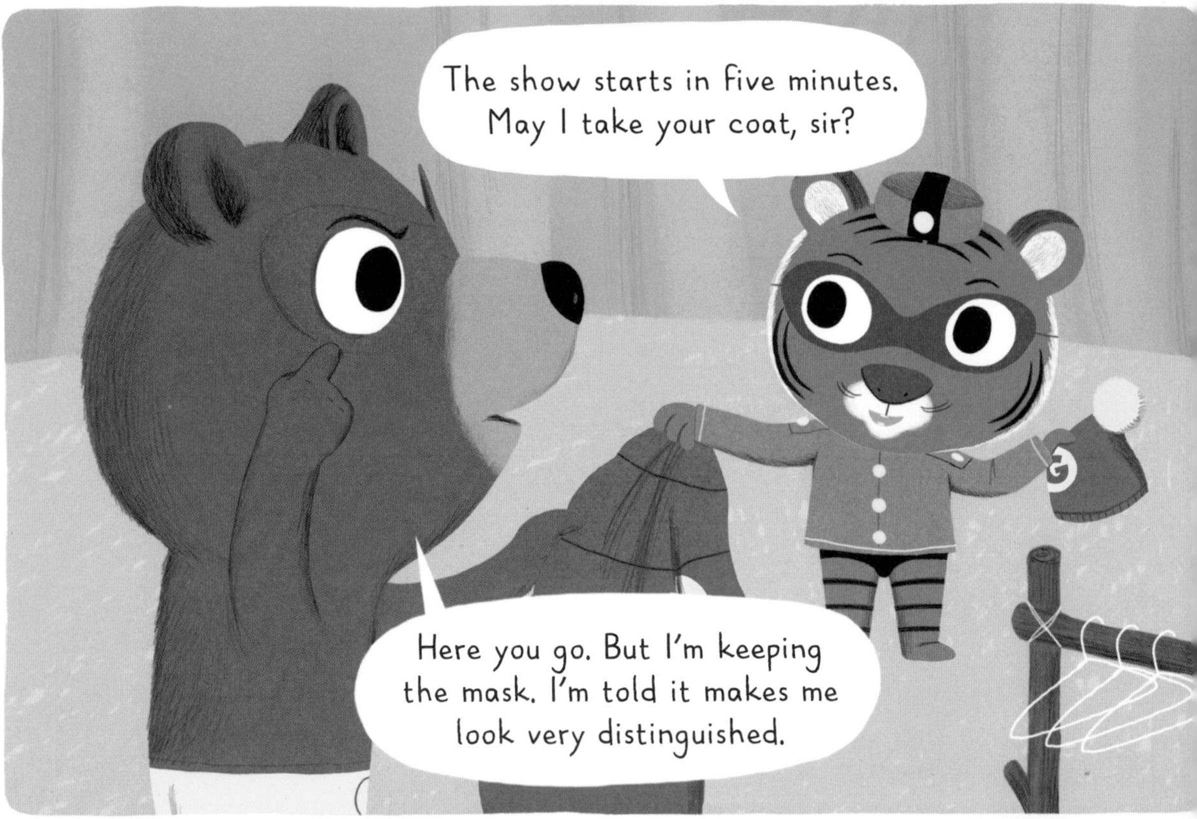
The show starts in five minutes. May I take your coat, sir?
Here you go. But I'm keeping the mask. I'm told it makes me look very distinguished.

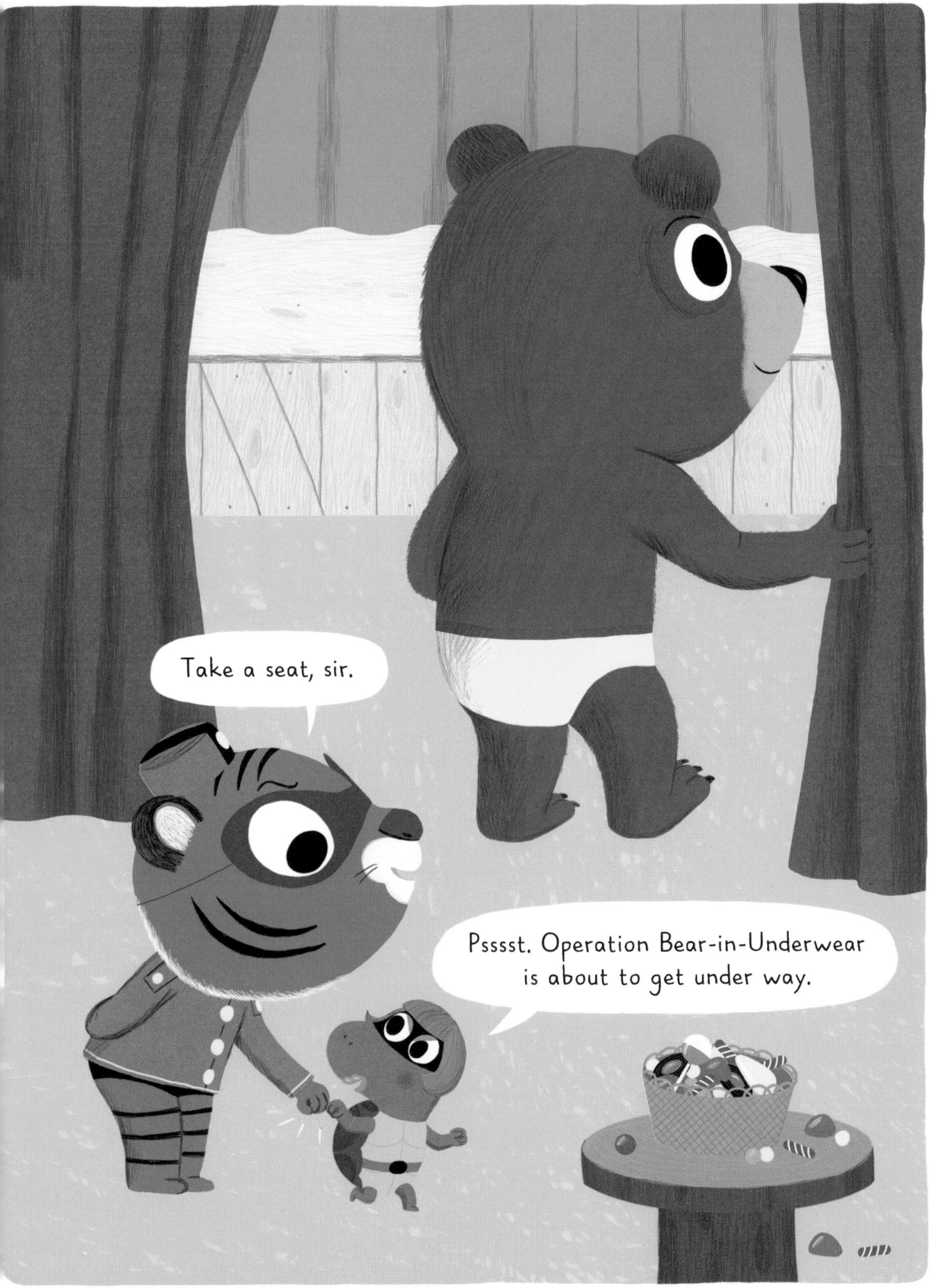
Take a seat, sir.
Psssst. Operation Bear-in-Underwear is about to get under way.

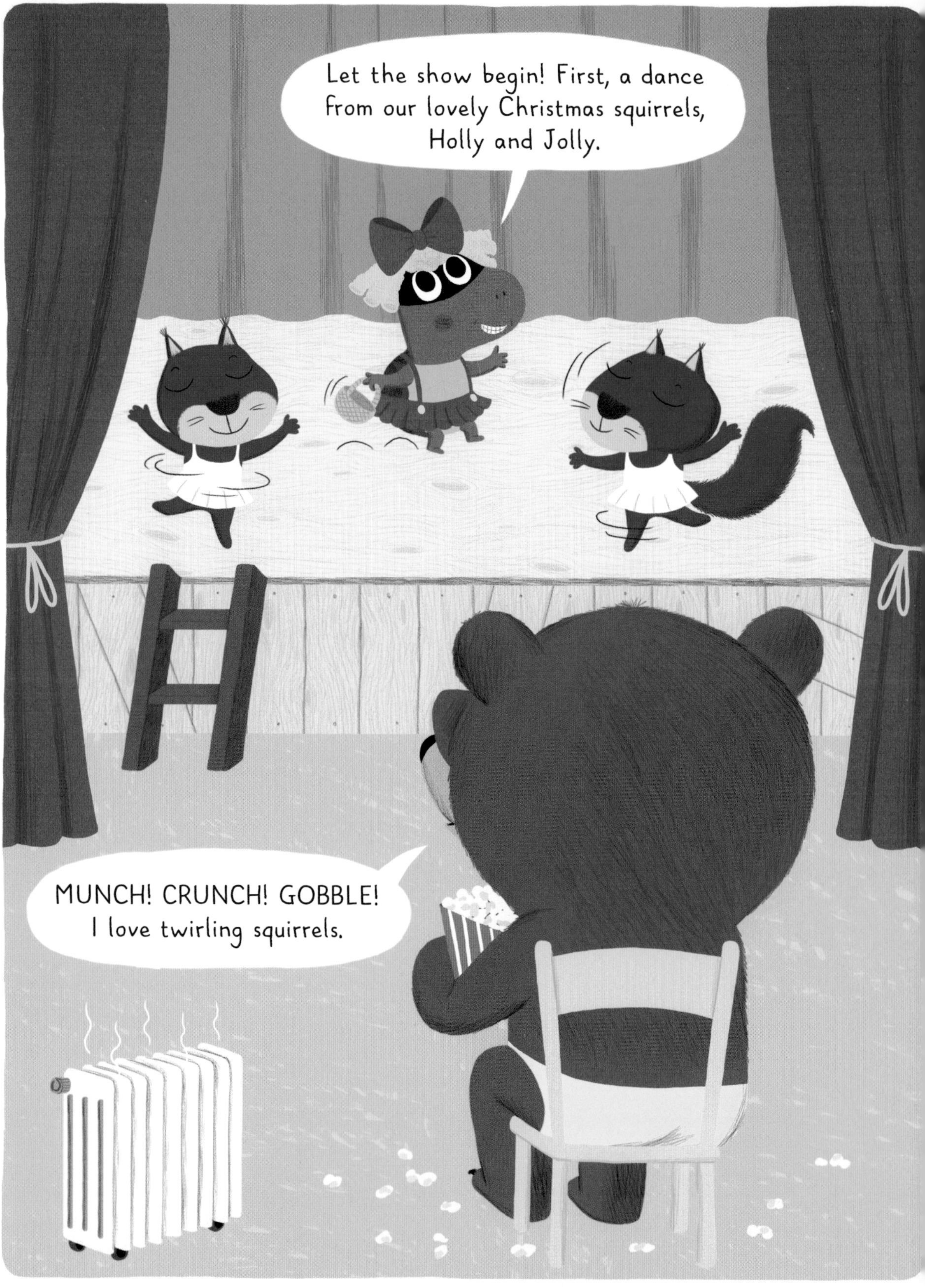
Let the show begin! First, a dance from our lovely Christmas squirrels, Holly and Jolly.
MUNCH! CRUNCH! GOBBLE! I love twirling squirrels.

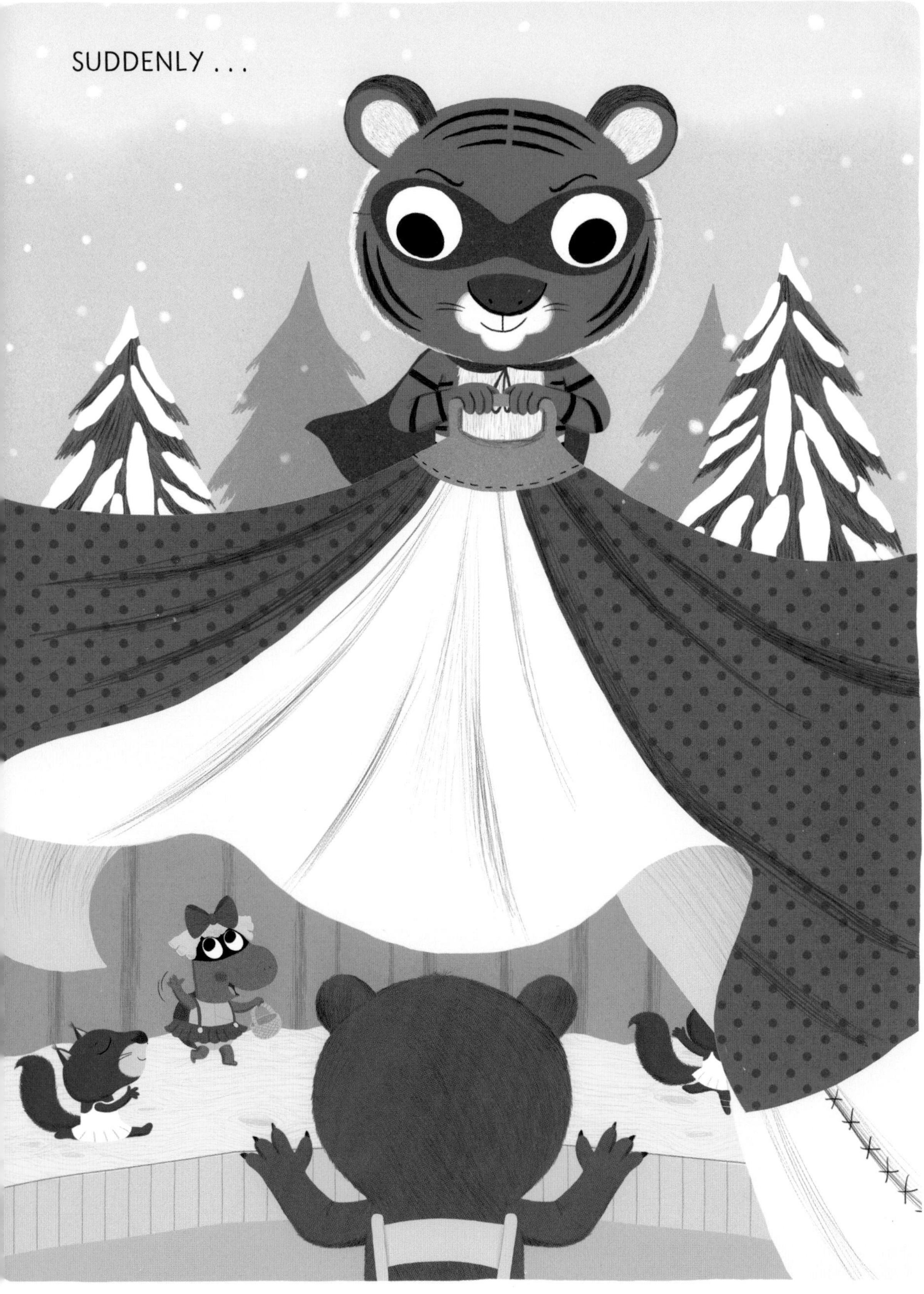
SUDDENLY . . .

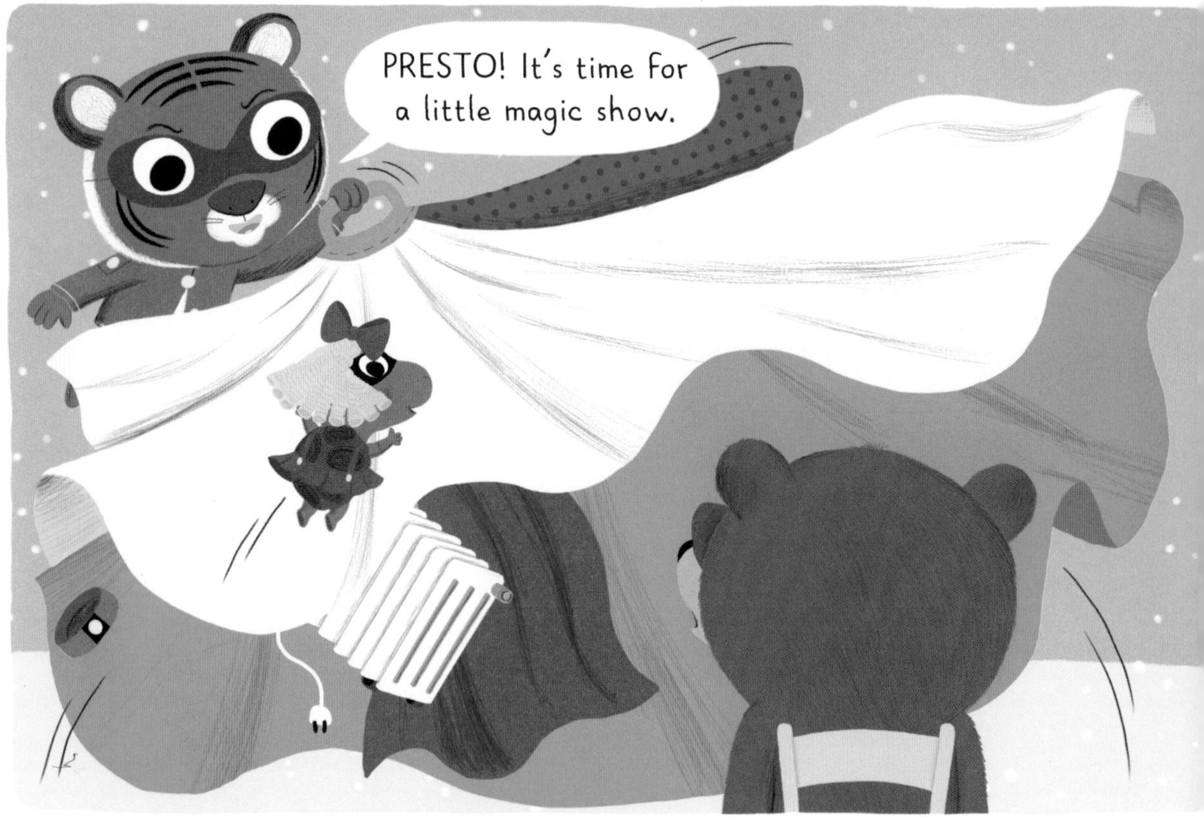
PRESTO! It's time for a little magic show.

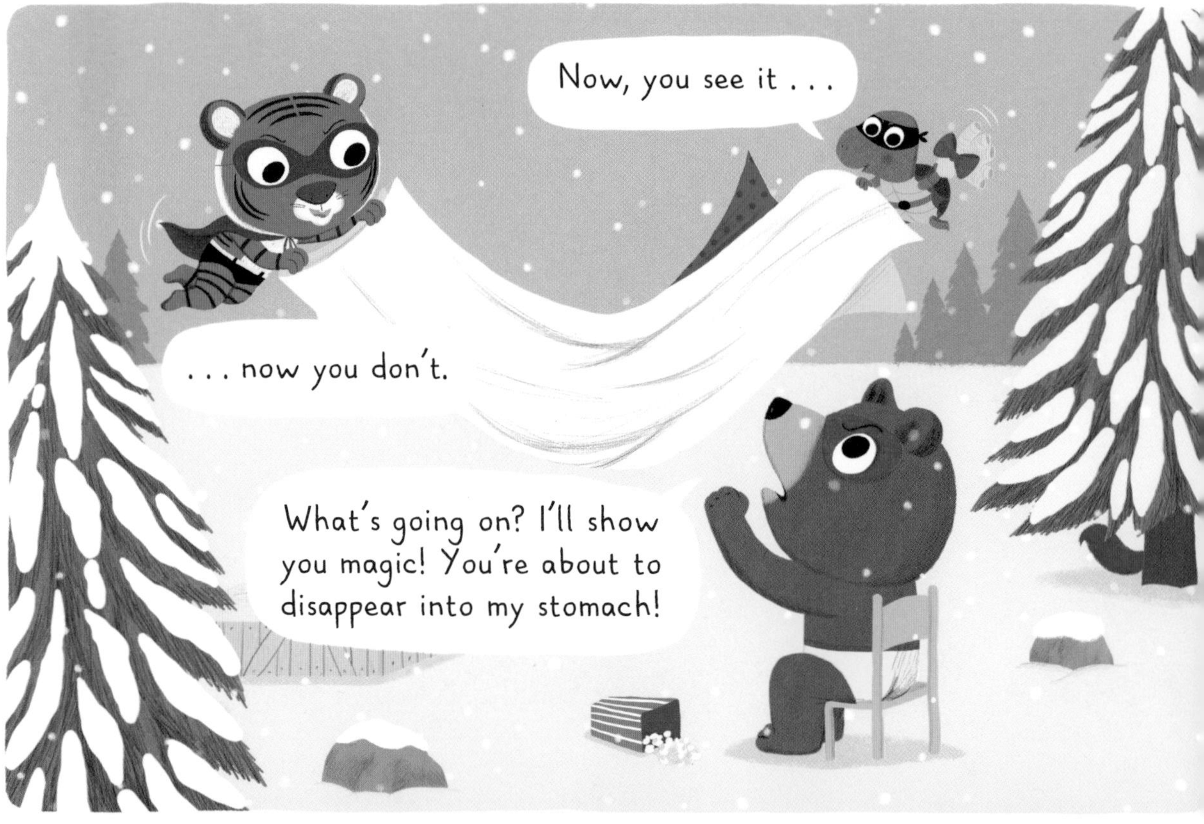
Now, you see it . . .
. . . now you don't.
What's going on? I'll show you magic! You're about to disappear into my stomach!

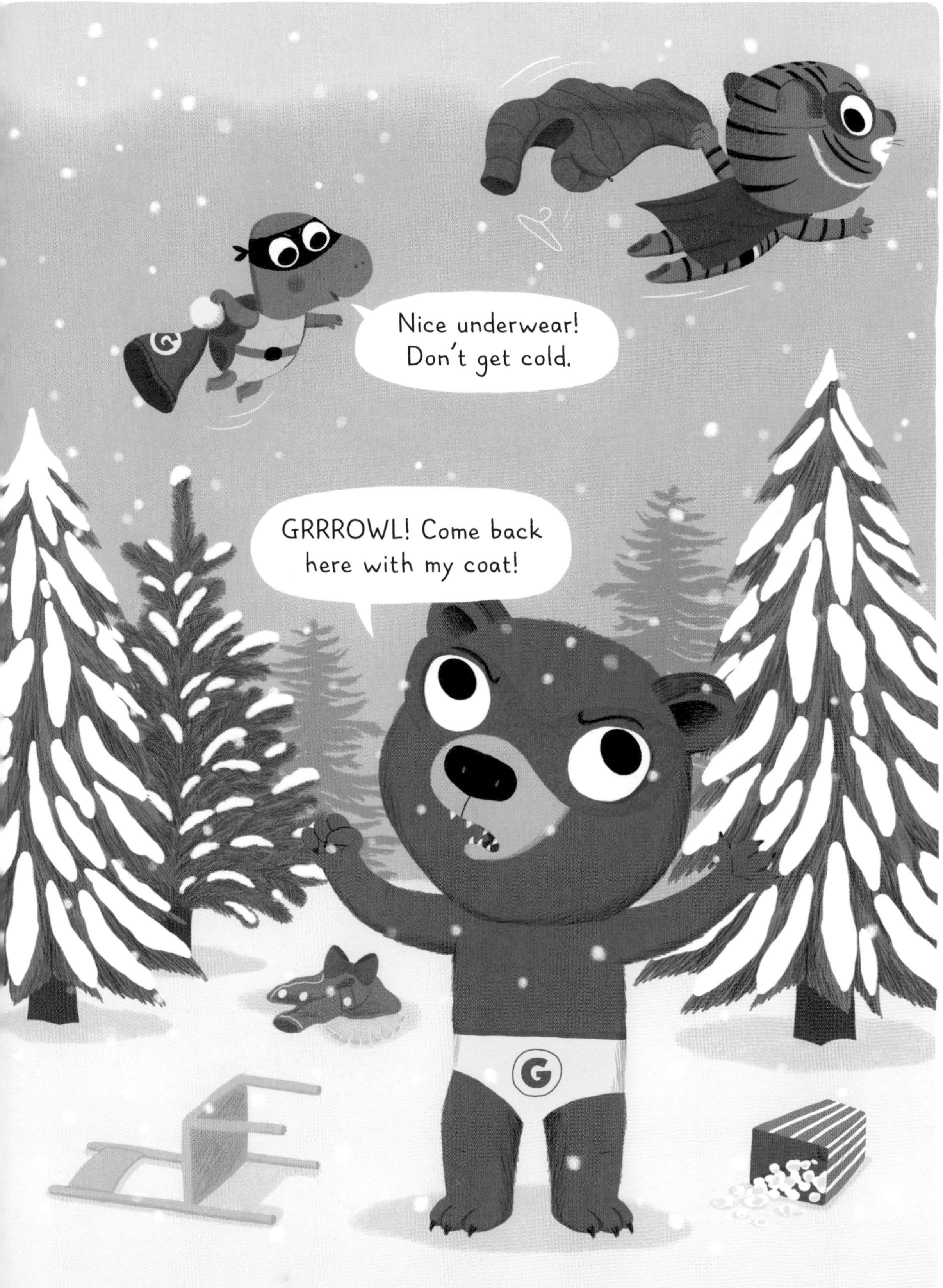
Nice underwear! Don't get cold.
GRRROWL! Come back here with my coat!

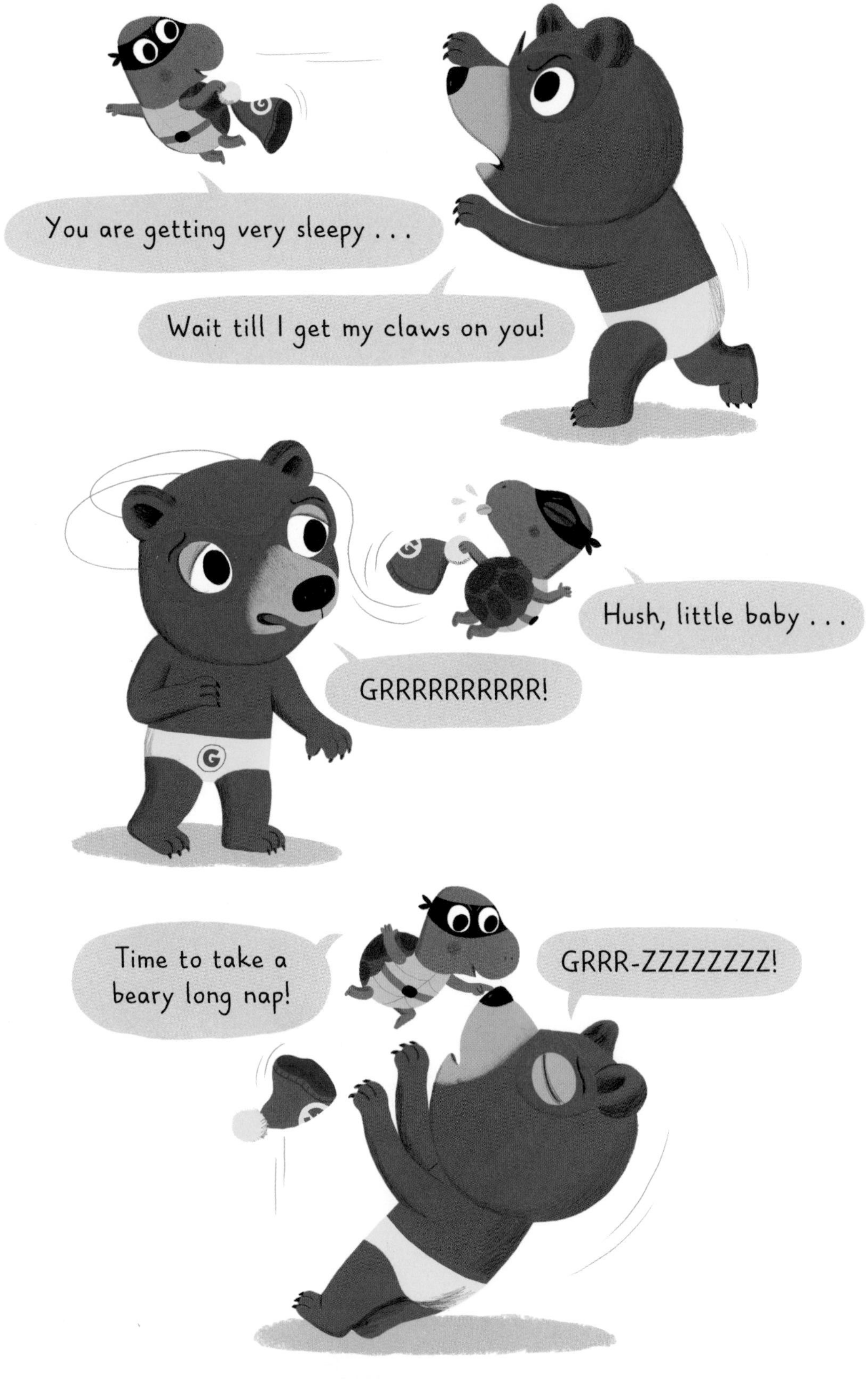
You are getting very sleepy . . .
Wait till I get my claws on you!
Hush, little baby . . .
GRRRRRRRRRR!
Time to take a beary long nap!
GRRR-ZZZZZZZZ!

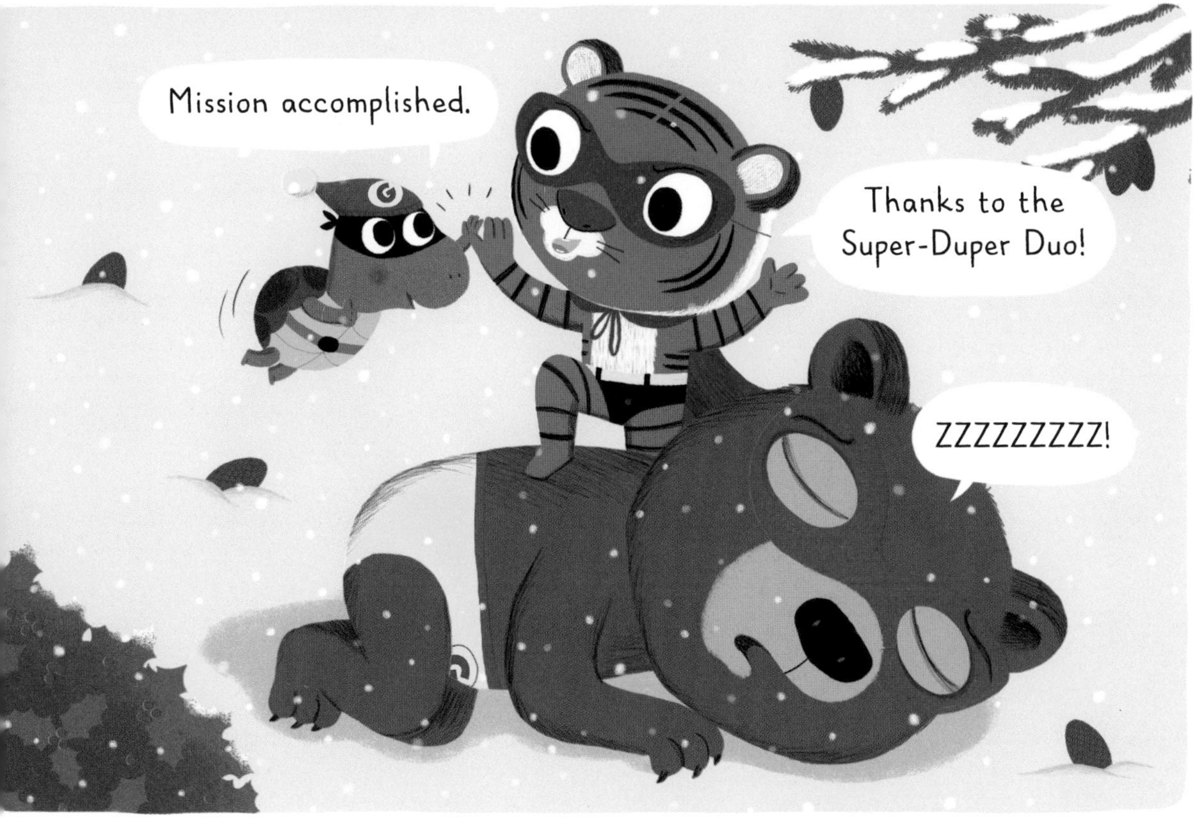
Mission accomplished.
Thanks to the Super-Duper Duo!
ZZZZZZZZZ!

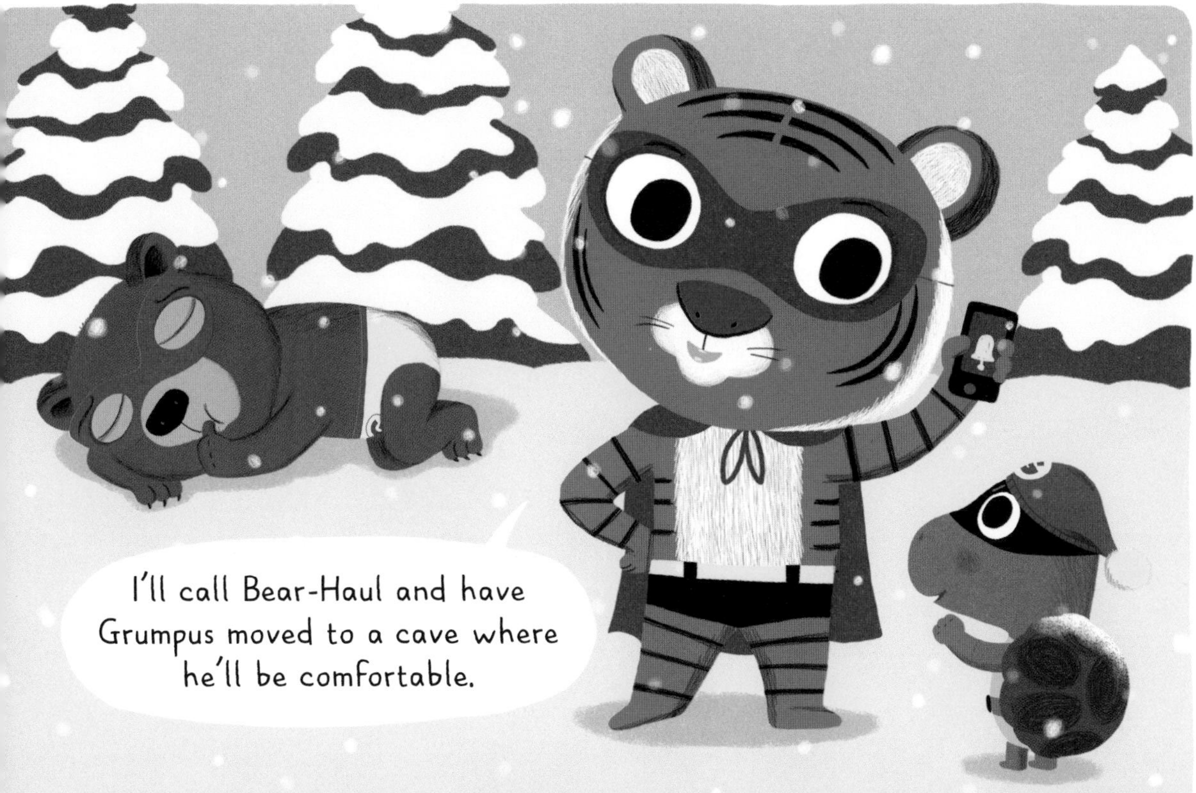
I'll call Bear-Haul and have Grumpus moved to a cave where he'll be comfortable.

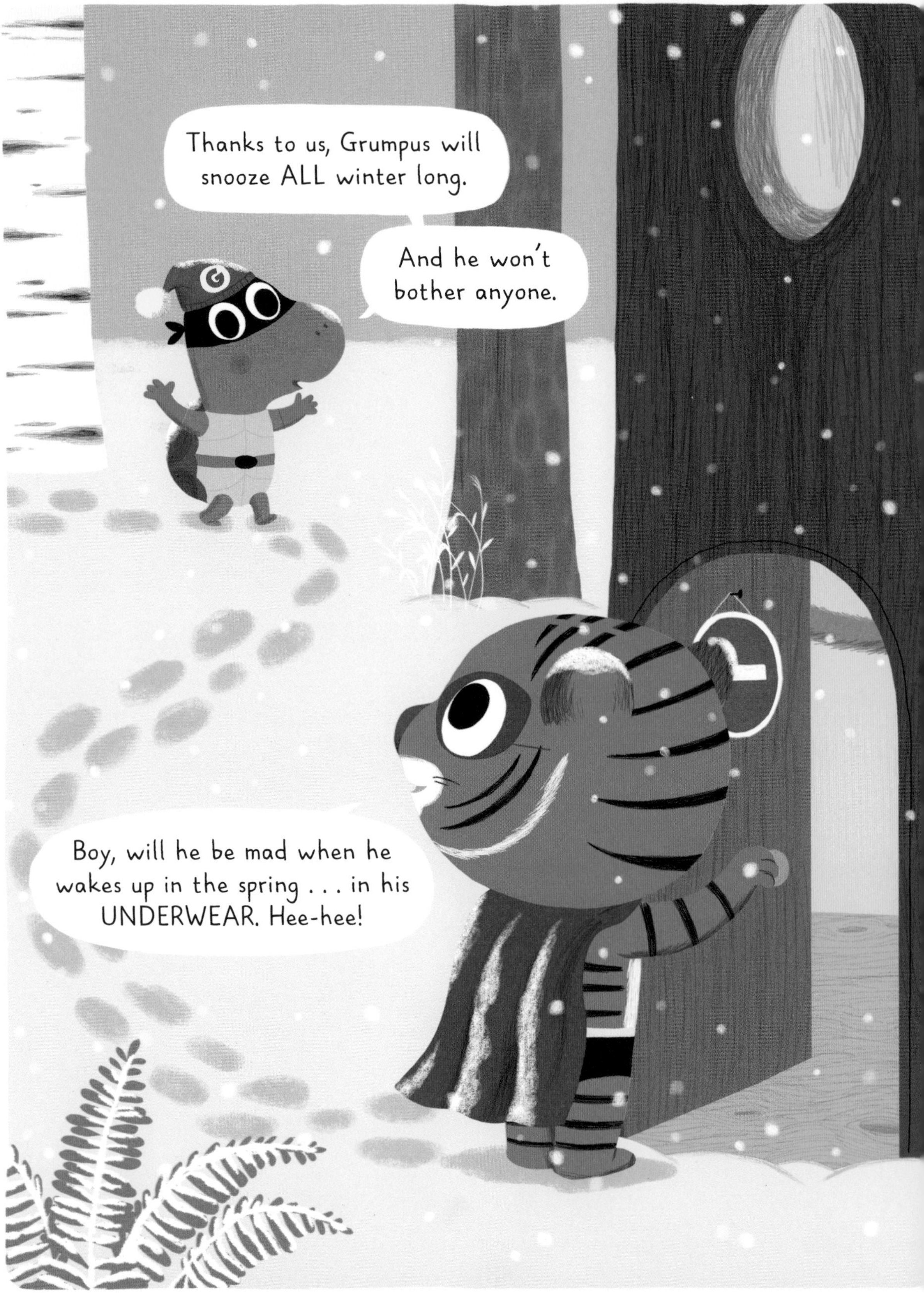
Thanks to us, Grumpus will snooze ALL winter long.
And he won't bother anyone.
Boy, will he be mad when he wakes up in the spring . . . in his UNDERWEAR. Hee-hee!

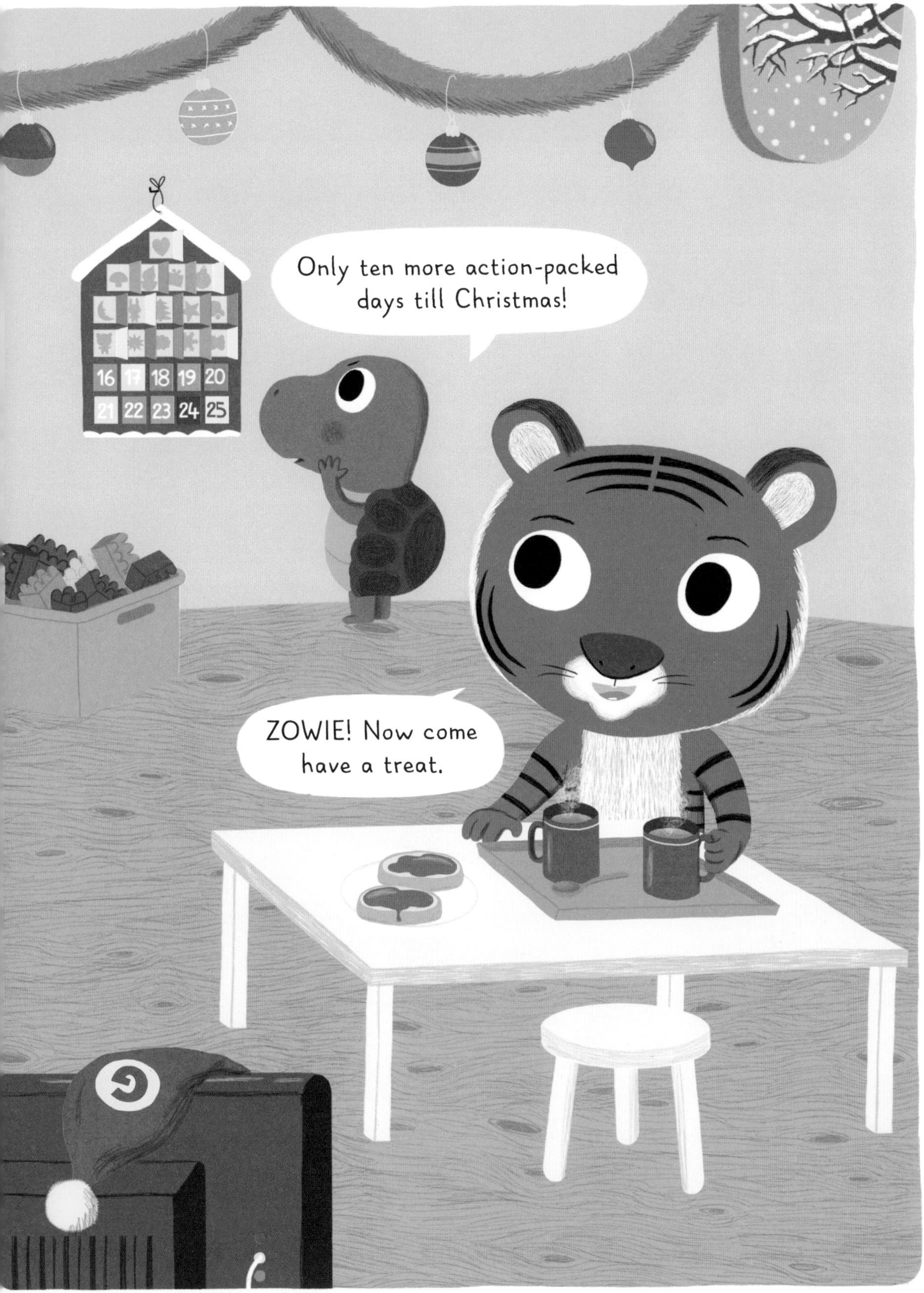
16 17 18 19 20
21 22 23 24 25
Only ten more action-packed days till Christmas!
ZOWIE! Now come have a treat.

SUPER-DUPER ANIMAL FACT

This Super-Duper Duo adventure features Grumpus, a cranky bear who needs to hibernate. As winter approaches, bears start eating a lot in order to fatten up. Then they curl up in a cave and fall into a deep slumber that lasts through the cold weather. This is called *hibernation*. Bears can live for many months off the food they ate, and they don't wake up until spring. Other animals also hibernate, such as hedgehogs and certain types of snakes and turtles. Now, that's a GRRREAT fact!